Snake *in the* Outhouse

and Other Stories

by Linda Banger

Photos by Bob Nandell

Published by
Sigler Printing & Publishing, Inc.
Ames, Iowa 50010-0887

Library of Congress Catalog Card Number: 98-060913
ISBN Number: 1-888223-12-X

Introduction

by Ed Sidey

If you were to pick out one decade in this century of momentous change and advancement as the best, what would it be? Would you cite the moment when man first flew? Or would you pick the time when mankind first set foot on the moon?

For me the choice is easy. As a country editor for more than half of our century, the best of times came right in the middle. It was the end of World War II, the best of times and for rural America, life was good. The boys were home, having defeated the two most fearsome professional military powers of the globe. They came back with little fanfare to farm and town alike and quietly took up civilian life again.

They rejoined a world where everything worked pretty well. On the farm, electricity plus gasoline and diesel power had removed much of the drudgery from farm labor. Better roads and better cars brought farm and town closer together. As rock roads replaced mud, the flickering light in the living rooms along country roads and town streets came not from candles or kerosene lanterns, but from TV tubes and the Ed Sullivan Show, which provided a common language and culture.

On the farm, soil conservation measures adopted in the desperate Dust Bowl years healed the erosion scars and restored some of the worn-out land. Farm size and farm populations were in a precarious balance. It was a time when many people had wrestled with greed and won the fight. The "get big or get out" philosophy had not yet taken charge.

Memories and stories of this golden age in rural America have been captured by Linda Banger as she lived them and wrote them in her own paper, "The New Virginian," and later in the Indianola Record-Herald. The life of a country editor leaves little time for reflection. Somewhere between selling advertising, gathering news, setting type and keeping books, Linda has managed in her columns to catch the glow of a time when front porches still graced the houses of town and country and families had time to use them. You will laugh at many of the stories, recall the sights, sounds and smells of others, and find your own recollections stimulated as you read, "Snake in the Outhouse and Other Stories." It is a slice of America that is gone, but thank goodness, not forgotten.

- Ed Sidey

Ed Sidey is Publisher Emeritus of the Adair County Free Press in Greenfield, Iowa, a newspaper that has been in the Sidey family for five generations. Even though he carries the title, "emeritus" he continues to write a weekly column, "Thoughts at Random," as well as editorials. He has been named a Master Editor-Publisher by the Iowa Newspaper Association, where he is a past president, as well as having served with distinction in many other capacities in that organization. He is a graduate of the School of Journalism at Iowa State University.

Foreword

by Jack Shelley

For some 25 years, as part of my role as News Director and principal newscaster of WHO, Des Moines, the 50,000-watt, clear-channel, "Voice of the Middle West," I aired a weekend newscast called, "The Home Town news."

The content was based on the personal, signed columns from scores of community newspapers - many of them weeklies with small circulations, but with a firm hand on the pulses of the little towns they served. Through those columns, I got to know about dozens of local characters, empathize with the hopes and dreams of hard-working midwesterners, and laugh at literally hundreds of yarns spun by the writers and editors. In almost 60 years of news work, I don't think I ever had more fun doing a broadcast series.

One reason why is that somewhere along the way I began to spot the writings of Linda Banger, and before long quotations from her columns were appearing again and again in "The Home Town News." As you read this book, you'll have no trouble seeing why.

Linda is the kind of down-to-earth, homey (but not cloying), often outrageously funny writer I sometimes think you can get only by mixing equal parts of northern Missouri and southern Iowa. There's Uncle Ken, getting rid of a snake in the outhouse with his trusty, 12-gauge shotgun. There's Grandpa Ozem Lachem Kingston, angrily using the kind of carbide found in miners' lamps to combat the crawdads. There's Great-Uncle Roscoe, who was buried with his brown felt fedora hat.

That is the kind of writing which comes from a person who has learned the hard way that life can be cruel but love can make it precious. From a woman whose mother somehow supported her family with the output of a 19-acre farm and a tiny check from the Veterans' Administration. From a writer with five children who has worked for newspapers of all sizes, but still lives on a farm in Warren County, Iowa.

I hope you'll enjoy Linda Banger's writings as much as I do. You'll find they have an unmistakable flavor from the heartland, a flavor as natural as that of the Missouri sorghum she tells you how to make.

- Jack Shelley

Jack Shelley is Professor Emeritus of Journalism and Mass Communication at Iowa State University, Ames, and a graduate of the School of Journalism of the University of Missouri, Columbia. Before joining the Iowa State faculty to head the program of broadcast journalism, Jack was on the staff of WHO Radio and Television in Des Moines, Iowa, for 30 years - 25 years as news director. The Des Moines Register, in a feature called "Iowa's Living Legends," called the voice of Jack Shelley "the most trusted in Iowa."

Acknowledgments

The stories in this book are about some of my memories and experiences while growing up in the country in the 1950s and early '60s, quite possibly the best time in the world to be a kid, and in one of the best places, the hills of north central Missouri, in Putnam County near Unionville.

Eventually, though, I grew up and left the nest, moved to the big city, married and began a family. Still, the call of the country never left me and soon my husband Bob, and I moved our young and growing family to a small farm south of Des Moines in Warren County, and there our children grew up.

Somewhere along the line I became involved in the world of journalism in a small, grassroots, community newspaper, The New Virginian, and later in the largest weekly in Iowa, the Indianola Record & Herald. My weekly newspaper column just sort of happened, and in it I've written of those growing-up years in Missouri and also of raising our five children on the place where we continue to live, and where now our grandchildren frolic when they visit.

And since most books contain thank-yous and acknowledgments, I can't let this moment pass without saying: Thank you to my husband Bob, the city-boy I married more than 30 years ago, who has always been supportive of me - he is my best friend, as well as sounding board, critic and proofreader. And to our kids, Mike, Tim, Rob, Jenny and Bethany, who have given me so many things to write about over the years, and who have grown into the warm, caring, giving and hard-working people I'm so proud of.

To my mom, who provided my brother, Mike, and me with such rich memories as we were growing up in what must often have been trying times. And adding to those memories and good times were a large assortment of extended family, as well as friends and neighbors who added to the richness of my life and gave me more stories to tell.

Thanks to friends and readers - and often the two seem to be one - as well as the fine staff at the Record-Herald, who help make this column happen each week.

To a group of people scattered across the Midwest - our friends and Bob's colleagues in the Midwest Area of the U.S. Postal Service, where he has been a proud employee for nearly 35 years: Your words of encouragement about this, my first book, not to mention the "When are you gonna have that book ready to read?" queries spurred me on to finally get it wrapped up and published.

To my pal, photographer Bob Nandell, thanks for your art which compliments my words. You are one of the best in the business. But thanks most of all for the photo which took 20 pounds off of me!

And two gentlemen who have my utmost respect, Ed Sidey and Jack Shelley: Your kind words of introduction made me feel quite humble, and that is not easily accomplished. You have added greatly to this work, and I hope you'll be proud of the finished product.

- Linda Banger

About The Author

Linda Banger writes a weekly column, "P.S. From Linda," for the Record-Herald & Indianola Tribune in Indianola, Iowa and has won a number of awards for her column from the National Newspaper Association and the Iowa Newspaper Association. Linda grew up in Putnam County, Missouri, near Unionville. She and her husband, Bob have raised their five children on a farm in Warren County, Iowa, near New Virginia.

For five years, 1978-83, she was the editor and publisher, indeed, the staff, of "The New Virginian," a weekly newspaper.

Table of Contents

My kids, all grown up. From the left: Rob, Jenny, Mike, Bethany and Tim.

Teething Rings & Printer's Ink

My daughters were home from college allowing us a chance to visit without watching long-distance phone charges. "What's with your column, Mom?" one of them asked. "You used to write about us kids and the family. Now you write about a bunch of other stuff and a lot of it I don't even know what you're talking about."

Well, there are a few who would agree with her, I thought, as I tried to explain the facts of writing a weekly column appealing to a wide range of readers of varying interests. "Exactly which part of the family should I write about?" I asked. "You're all grown and scattered out now and not a part of our daily household. And considering what I've seen of university life when we've visited you at the University of Iowa I'm not real sure I want to know what all goes on there, let alone share it with readers."

But her question got me thinking about how this column has evolved over 18 years, because that's how long it has appeared in print every week in our little corner of the world.

It was October 1978 when it first saw the light of day, and then merely by accident.

Six months earlier, in a surge of cabin fever mixed with baby blues and boredom, I had gotten into the newspaper business.

The long winter was nearly over - the weather had been cold and drizzly for weeks - and I had five children under the age of 11. After being pregnant for two years, my youngest kids were Jenny, who was 17 months old, and Bethany, who was four months old. The three boys Mike, Tim and Robbie, ranged in age from 6 to 11.

One day the mail brought the local paper, The New Virginian, with the announcement that it was closing its doors and going out of business. "What a shame," I thought. "I'll bet I could put out a pretty good little newspaper by myself doing it here at home."

And that's how I entered the world of journalism, and by ironic timing my first day was April Fool's Day. Learning as I went along and through trial and error, with equipment regularly breaking down, late hours, tears, headaches, exhaustion, teething tots and the other complexities of juggling a large family along with a budding "career," I got through the first weeks and months. The small eight-page paper was printed at the Record-Herald and Indianola Tribune with its great staff. The publisher was Lew Kimer, God rest his kind soul. He was my newspaper godfather, so to speak.

Most of the news going into the paper was community and school news and unedited press releases. At the time, I wasn't aware that as editor (also publisher, reporter, advertising, composition and circulation manager) I could actually chop up releases to fit into whatever space might accommodate them to to avoid mind-numbing, unreadable blather.

It was that fall when I had established a routine of sorts and was more comfortable with deadlines mixed with diaper changes, suppertime and Cub Scout meetings that I began to write a column. It came at a time when a couple of things happened and I wanted to write about them. But what I had in mind didn't quite fit into what I was familiar with: press releases, obituaries or correspondents' items of community news. So I wrote my thoughts and not wanting to appear pushy or self-important, I put my article on the last page of the paper. As an inveterate letter-writer, I titled the piece with the only thing which occurred to me: "P.S. From Linda," and that was the beginning.

Ironically, given my daughter's recent comments, the column was not about my family. It was an opinion piece about the deaths of two men - each died on the same day. One, Pope John Paul I, was mourned the world over. The other man's death was remarked by few. A lot of people in Warren County knew him, but he was thought by many to be a cranky old nut. But my family knew him to be a crusty yet decent, old eccentric and on occasion he could even be sweet. Russell Wright had been our next-door neighbor during our first years on the farm. In fact, we bought our place from him, and he continued to live next door in a small, cluttered trailer amidst a collection of pets, beasts and junk. Every cat and dog in a 30-mile radius knew him, and every kid around could count on him for a Tootsie Pop.

One day I noticed I hadn't seen him out and about in his usual routine. My husband, Bob, checked on him and found him unconscious. He had suffered a stroke and was later moved to a nursing home on the other side of the state where he died. I wrote about him because he had been a kind and interesting person, and I felt something should be said about him and some of his life's stories as he had told us.

The next week there was something else deserving comment and the next and the next. And so it's continued 52 weeks a year since.

I got out of the newspaper business five years after getting into it. But not for long as it turned out. Almost immediately I was approached about writing a column for the RHT. Whoa, the big time! From a small community paper to the largest weekly in Iowa? Okay, I'd give it a shot.

This column became a journal of sorts on my growing and changing family. Not just the kids at home, but the extended family of parents, grandparents, cousins; of anniversaries, class reunions, deaths, family traditions and memories of growing up in Missouri in the good old days of the 1950s and 60s.

My kids virtually grew up in this column as I've shared them with readers. They teethed, learned table manners, went on their first rabbit-hunting trips, appeared in church plays, had their first driving lessons - followed by their first car wrecks. Graduations, marriages and the arrival of our first grandchildren have been chronicled here.

Occasionally, I have gone on an opinion-sortie since there is little that goes on in the world around us that does not affect me and mine. And like many, there is very little on which I don't have an opinion. The only difference between me and most people is I weave my opinions into words on a newspaper page to be agreed with or not.

And since I was raised as I was - in a one-parent household of extremely modest means by a conservative Southern Baptist mother and other adults around me where of a similar nature, more likely than not my opinion is conservative.

Now that my last chick has left the nest, the stories to write about my kids and their adventures, or of regular day to day household life have become more sparse. So I share my thoughts on events going on around Warren County, the state, the nation, the world - indeed, I may go intergalactic.

And to my kids not understanding what I'm writing about: Open a newspaper, watch a news broadcast or talk to people around you. because it's there you'll surely find the grist for forming opinions about the changing world you're growing up in.

Or I could always turn to writing a recipe column. For chicken soup, start with a pot of water.....

At the right, Uncle Kenneth, the snake-slayer. My brother Mike and cousin Sandy are at the left.

Snake In The Outhouse

My son came home one afternoon from his job on a neighboring farm. He'd been doing field work, he said, and had come upon the biggest old bullsnake he'd ever seen.

The hair raised from my neck as he described the snake's head flattening, spreading out and looking "real weird." That didn't sound like any bullsnake to me, and another neighbor concurred, suggesting that Mike had found a spreading viper, the name of which even sounds dreadful, lethal, and so snakily reptilian and scaly it gives me the creeps. Oooh, I hate snakes.

I hadn't thought of spreading vipers for ages, figuring, I guess, that they were native to Missouri. Or that their legend had, in fact, been blown out of all proportion by solicitous, caring parents who terrify their young children with tales of ravenous serpents loose in the woods. The stories will give the kids nightmares, but they will stay closer to the house.

My cousin, Sue, though, can testify that spreading vipers can be found close to home. Sue was the oldest of my Uncle Kenneth's family who lived right across the field from us when we were kids. Sue and I were the same age and best friends, besides being blood kin.

Our families lived near enough to each other that everyone could hear fights or shouts of triumph and laughter; or sibling spats and screams of outrage. We kids could shout back and forth to one another either hurling teasing insults or making plans for adventures during school vacation.

Living that close all those years, we became attuned to one another's lifestyles and habits.

One of Sue's daily goals was to try to get out of helping her sister, Sandy, do the supper dishes. To attain this goal she would from time to time pull the "call of nature" trick. This was back in the days before most farm homes had indoor plumbing.

Sandy would begin washing the dishes. "I've gotta go the the bathroom," Sue would announce as she threw down the dish towel, bolted out the back door and headed down the path to the little house. It so happened that there was a convenient stack of comic books for a kid's reading enjoyment in the little house. Hours could be spent reading comics while avoiding helping a sister with the dishes.

On one particular late afternoon Cousin Sue followed her ritual of visiting the little house during dishwashing time. She left the door ajar to catch a nice breeze and then comfortably seated herself and commenced to read a comic book or leaf through a Sears & Roebuck catalog while Sandy wailed over the dishpan about the unfairness of it all.

Across the field my mom and I were outdoors and I suppose my brother was probably out in the yard wearing his Davy Crockett hat and fighting off Indians.

Then in the stillness of a rural Missouri twilight as the frogs began croaking and the crickets were chirping, we heard Sue let out a blood-curdling scream from the vicinity of the little house. We heard Kenneth kick the kitchen door open and yell out, "What'n the hell's goin' on out there?!?!"

"Daddy, Daddy, help!" we heard Sue shout. "There's a big snake in here!"

The next sounds we heard were those of pounding and breaking wood and then the roar of Kenneth's double-barreled shotgun.

We dropped what we were doing and ran across the field to find out what was going on. Sue was crying, Kenneth was swearing, Sue's mom, Virginia, was trying to comfort little Joe Dean, and Sandy, with sudsy hands, was standing back looking rather smug.

The story came out. While Sue was sitting in the little house answering the call of nature and reading the comic book, a large mean-looking snake - an evil spreading viper - slithered in through the doorway.

Sue dropped the comic, grabbed her drawers, levitated onto the quaint bench-type seat of the two-holer and began screaming for her dad. Kenneth came running with the 12-gauge, aimed it down at the snake and told Sue to get out of the way. She did just that by leaping out through the open doorway, soaring over the snake and landing behind her dad. Kenneth shot the snake using both barrels, vaporized the serpent, blew out the floor of the outhouse and landed on his butt from the kick of the shotgun.

It wasn't long after all this excitement that Sue's family had indoor plumbing installed.

The new bathroom was a great convenience, of course, but it lacked the solitude of the old one. A person couldn't take their ease while reading great literature of the day.

But Sandy had help with the supper dishes from then on.

"Blest be the ties that bind." The George Hunt family, from left: Kenneth, Great-Grandpa George, Roscoe, Ruth, Thelma, Mary Phyllis, Isabella, my grandma, Hallie, Celeste. Circa 1953

We buried my great-uncle Roscoe on a wintry, blustery morning last week.

People sometimes underestimate the value of relatives like the "greats" - great-niece, great-nephew, great-grandparents, great-aunts or uncles. These relatives usually are either so distant or so old that we don't know them well or never knew them at all.

But since my mother is an only child and my dad had only one sister, my great-uncles are all I ever had in the way of older male relatives who were not my grandfathers.

My great-uncles were my grandmother's younger brothers.

They came from a large Irish family, the children of George and Nellie Hunt. My great-grandparents, George and Nellie, had 14 children, including my grandmother, Hallie. The names of six of their young ones are inscribed on a memorial stone in the cemetery in my hometown. The others, Isabella, Thelma, Celeste, Mary Phyllis, Ruth, Kenneth and Roscoe, were the great aunts and uncles I was fortunate to grow up knowing. Thelma, Celeste and Mary Phyllis moved west many years before I was born - Thelma and Mary Phyllis to California, and Celeste to Utah. Thelma became a much-married-and-divorced wealthy, real estate agent. She had no children. However, she made regular trips back to the Missouri home place to visit the family.

She would stay at our place or my grandparents' and it was always a treat when she pulled in the drive in her big Caddy convertible. She wore expensive knit dresses, high platform shoes with rhinestone heels, huge earrings and brooches, and always had her mink stole with her - even in the barn lot when she tip-toed around visiting with us at chore time. She lolled around the house until noon in her nightgown and negligee, much to our scandalized delight. Her companion when in Missouri was always a man named Ralph. I was probably a teen-ager before I learned that Ralph had been her first - or perhaps second - husband. Thelma died a few years ago, survived by her fifth - or perhaps it was sixth - husband, whom she had loved well enough to marry and divorce and then remarry years later.

Ruth lived in the next county when I was a kid. She was a somewhat cranky, chain-smoking, cynical person, but I remember she could be quite kind.

Isabella was a school teacher in Missouri for years. She was probably approaching retirement when she divorced her husband of many years (a man who delighted in teasing and tormenting kids - I loathed him) and moved to California to join her daughter. She later remarried and is now deceased.

Mary Phyllis and Celeste paid less frequent visits back home, but they had families to look after out west. Both were devout Mormans. Celeste died last year in Utah. Mary Phyllis, a retired nurse and the family genealogist, is unwell and lives with her daughter in California. Besides my grandmother who is 92 and in a nursing home, she is the only one now remaining of George and Nellie's children.

One of my favorite relatives in the whole world was my great-uncle Kenneth. He and his family lived across the field from us at the old home place, my great-grandfather's house. Kenneth was a rascally soul and had a certain fondness for the bottle. But in my one-parent home he was always there to help us. He was the one my mom usually turned to when she needed some advice or a man's help. He is the one who put chains on the car and drove through an ice storm and blizzard to take my mom and brother to the hospital when my brother had a ruptured appendix. His kids were my age, and his daughters, Sue and Sandy, were as close as if they were my sisters. They still are.

He is the one who went to the sheriff when my mentally-ill dad became dangerously abusive and needed to be committed to the state hospital.

Kenneth was a friend and an ally to a kid. That is, until I messed up, sassed back or caused any worry for my mom. He never laid a hand on me, but he could lecture or give that certain withering, shame-inducing Hunt-look.

Then there was Roscoe. Roscoe and his wife, Emma, lived across the county near Ruth. But their home was a frequent stop in the family-visiting ritual. They had a large family - most of their kids were much older than me. Basil Dean, Betty and George are my elders by 10 to 15 years; the twins, Ronald and Donald, are three years older than me, although when you're a little kid that may as well be 20 years. Melanie was the family surprise and came much later - in fact she is 10 years younger than me.

Roscoe, too, was a stabilizing influence in my kidhood. He also looked after my mama and helped out when a man's help was needed. He was with my grandpa when they came to south Missouri to help my mother move us back to northern Missouri when my dad's illness resulted in his first hospitalization. Of that long trip I remember only being jammed into some vehicle crowded with household goods. But I remember Roscoe being there, and how nice and safe it felt to be with him.

Roscoe and Emma were around on many of the Saturday afternoons when the whole family sometimes seemed to congregate on the town square. He would join my grandpa and and my Uncle Kenneth in the tavern while the women of the family did their shopping. I can remember a few times being sent into the tavern to retrieve my male relatives. Women weren't generally seen going into such places on a Saturday afternoon, but it was acceptable for a kid to go in to deliver a message.

And, of course, we were always together on Memorial Day at the cemetery, always meeting up at the Hunt plot, and later at the annual family reunion.

Roscoe and Emma had been at my parents' wedding in 1941 and a few years later were at my great-grandparents' the evening I decided to enter the world - that was when my mom was staying there because Daddy was in the Army and my grandparents, with whom she lived, were on a mud road. One evening my mom thought she had a bad stomach ache from eating the grapes that ripen in September. Emma told her sagely that her stomach ache had not been caused by grapes, and she and Roscoe took Mama to the hospital, where I was born a few hours later.

Roscoe and Emma were at my wedding, held in my grandparents' living room where my mom and dad had been married. In turn, I was at their golden wedding anniversary celebration in 1980 - indeed, their lives have threaded through my own.

The past six years, suffering from Alzheimer's Disease, Roscoe was in a nursing home - the same place as my grandmother. It was a touching yet heartbreaking sight to see this elderly brother and sister together, she in a wheelchair and unable to walk, and he with diminishing intellect.

Roscoe was buried with his brown felt fedora hat. I remember that hat and his wearing it at a jaunty angle. I remember with love and respect my great-uncle, Roscoe Basil Hunt. And as always with fond memories, the person who left them will not soon be forgotten.

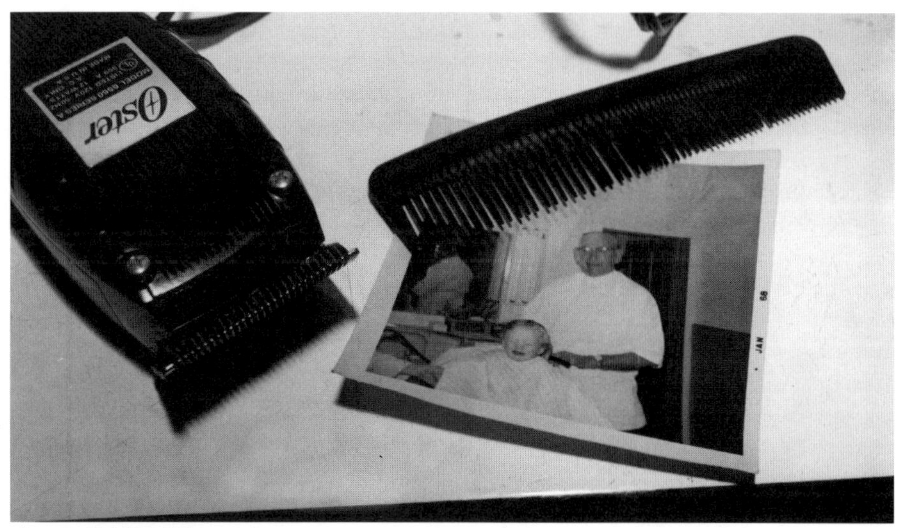

photo by Bob Nandell

Family Barber

An article about barber shops I read recently reminded me of just what an important role a barber and his shop can play in the life of a family. A man might lose his dentist, his family doctor, a stockbroker or a favorite golf partner, but a real blow would be to lose his barber.

When I was a young girl, female-type persons did not visit barbers except to wait for a male relative to be groomed, in my case a brother, or on rare occasions to accompany my grandpa to get his hair cut. Our family barber was Ed Guffey.

Ed's shop was a wonderland of dog-eared comic books and magazines; of strange good smells of hair tonic, cigar and pipe smoke; of cuspidors and curious-looking ash trays.

Saturday afternoons, probably once a month or when my brother became shaggy-looking, he would go to Ed's barber shop. It was a ritual that never varied.

When my brother was just a little boy my mom would take him by the hand and we would all visit the shop together. Ed would bring his booster board out, place it across the arms of the barber chair and set my brother on it. He would work on Mike's hair with clippers and then scissors and a comb with the snip-snip sounds accompanying the hum of a fan in the background. Family news was exchanged as well as local news between Ed and Mama and any of the other people waiting for the chair, or perhaps they were just killing a Saturday afternoon.

The barber shop was always a popular place for men to loaf if they were waiting on wives to shop or kids to return from the movie matinee, or for no particular reason at all except it was a hospitable place.

I never remember Ed looking any different for all the years I knew him; he had a plump, pink face, white hair, silver-framed glasses, and always wore a white buttoned-at-the-shoulder barber's shirt. Always appearing neat and unrumpled, he was a gentle, cheerful man, and I never heard him say a mean word about anyone.

With my brother's hair cut, Ed would bring out a soft brush and sweep off the clippings, put a little talcum powder around Mike's neck, and apply some pinkish hair oil that smelled sweet and perfumey.

The shop had all kinds and shapes of bottles filled with good-smelling oils and tonics and lotions setting near the large mirror behind the barber chair. My brother remembers pictures of Dizzy Dean and Pee Wee Reece hanging on the wall. Ed was a great baseball fan and he was usually tuned into a game being broadcast on the radio which he kept in the shop.

As my brother grew up, he and his buddies visited the barber shop on Saturday afternoons after the matinee movie; or after they were in high school, before important events like prom or graduation. Later still, stopping in and visiting with Ed and any of the older fellows who happened to be in the shop was a must-do when a young man came home on leave from the service or from far-away places. What Ed must've thought as he watched the boys whose hair he'd trimmed since they were little as they grew up into men.

I don't remember if Ed was still in business when my brother got out of the Marines and grew his hair down to his waist and drove a Volkswagen van. I imagine not.

Ed gave my oldest son one of his first haircuts, and I have a picture of them still, Ed poised with comb and scissors, his pinkie extended, and my son's little-boy face scrunched up because falling hair was tickling his nose.

That was probably one of the only haircuts any of my sons received in a barber shop because I've been cutting their hair since I bought my first set of clippers for a dollar at a garage sale.

In their tender years they weren't wise enough to be alarmed or to raise objections to a haircut in the kitchen. And their blonde locks fell to the floor as I gave them butch haircuts in the summer and neatly trimmed hair with side parts for school. I'd wet their hair down, part it on the side and brush it back neatly. They looked so sweet.

By the time they were old enough to know any better I'd become skilled enough at cutting hair that there were rarely really noticeable mishaps with the haircuts. Oh, every now and then a boy would move the wrong way and the clippers would dig a little deeper and leave a distinct cleft, but I felt it gave the haircut character. Barbers these days charge extra for those little touches.

As my boys became older they began mentioning the word "style" and wanted their hair shaped rather than cut. I pointed out to them that if they wanted it that way, they were welcome to shuck out $15 or more and have it "styled" somewhere else.

They remained faithful kitchen-barber clients of mine.

Bob, too, as he watched me become more accomplished, began having me cut his hair.

I've become familiar with every swirl, cowlick, double-crown, curl and lock on the heads of my guys. What began as a purely practical gesture on my part, has continued as a convenience. It is, after all, easier to burst into the house and say, "Mom, I need a haircut - have you got time?" whether it's 10 in the morning or at night, weekday or holiday.

Still, I sometimes feel I've robbed them of an American birthright, the tradition of visiting the barber. I remember the day our youngest son came home from college with a haircut that gave his dad and me a start. His hair had been cut in its usual short style, but as he turned his head we noticed it looked as if a two-bottom plow had been dropped on his head, going around over his ears and coming to points at the nape of his neck. His buddy had given him a haircut, he announced. "I didn't know he was going to be a barber," I said.

"He's not," Robbie replied, "He's going to be a dentist."

Candy Supper

When I was a young girl attending a one-room school in the hills of north-central Missouri, there was an event in the fall that we looked forward to almost as much as Christmas. And that was the annual candy supper, a fund-raising event that combined the rituals of a neighborhood social with that of an amateur theatrical. It was one of THE social highlights of the year in our rural community and aroused all the fervor of a Baptist revival.

For the unfortunates who have never heard of a candy supper, allow me to enlighten you.

Each female planning to attend the event, be she five or 90, would make or buy a box of candy and wrap it in pretty paper and ribbons. Arriving at the schoolhouse for the candy supper, the box of sweets would be furtively placed on a table with other boxes of candy. The boxes were later auctioned off to sons, husbands, cousins, boyfriends and only rarely brothers, although in a pinch they were acceptable bidders.

The man or boy who bid on a box of candy didn't know whose candy he was buying, (which generally made for some interesting speculations) UNLESS a girl would tell her best friend which box of candy was hers and the friend would in turn reveal the identity to her brother and the word was passed along until it reached the right set of ears. The candy buyee and the candy buyer would in this manner be correctly paired up and true romance was helped along.

At school, preparations for the candy supper began weeks in advance. Raffle tickets for a gen-u-ine Indian blanket were sold to every relative, friend, neighbor or stranger a kid could come across. The tickets were homemade on Big Chief tablet paper and sold for 10 cents each or three for a quarter. If a kid was real lucky she would find someone who had either been drinking in town on a Saturday afternoon and was feeling generous, or maybe they'd just gotten their milk check cashed. That student might sell as much as a dollar's worth of tickets to one person!

As the big night approached, a cleaning spree was carried out at school. The blackboard was washed and new chalk was laid out. The little first graders were sent outdoors to clean the erasers against the stuccoed sides of the school. The coal stove was cleaned out and fresh sweeping compound was thrown down. The curtains were dragged out of boxes and the wrinkles shaken out. Then with the use of No. 9 wire, hog rings and safety pins, the curtains were strung across one end of the school room. They were a drab, sleazy gray fabric made by someone's mother on a treadle sewing machine, but in our eyes they were just as grand as the red velvet ones at the Royal Movie Theater on the town square.

Finally, the night arrived. The school was clean and the last rehearsal had been held. Construction paper pilgrims, pumpkins and turkey decorations on the walls and crepe paper ceiling streamers transformed the familiar schoolroom into an enchanted theatrical palace.

The kids were dressed in their best clothes and a nervous teacher greeted parents at the door. At a signal from the teacher, the students went to their places behind the curtains. The audience settled in their seats, snuffled their noses and cleared their throats one last time. Silence. It was time for The Program to begin.

The littlest kids would shyly recite their simple little "pieces," and there were plays and skits by older classes. Solos, duets, trios, and/or quartets of folk ballads ("Oh where have you been, Billy boy, Billy boy? Oh where have you been charming Billy?") and patriotic hymns were performed. The Spence sisters had their accordions and the old upright piano, always in need of tuning, also was put to use.

Parents proudly sat in the audience at the students' desks beaming at their talented offspring. Nudges and winks were abundant and little prompting was needed from the teacher as the eye contact between mother and child, with mother mouthing the oft-rehearsed lines, was all the help needed. Encouraging nods, a big grin, a frown when memory failed, a look of triumph when the piece was finished and then the applause - a polite stiff bow, and the curtains were closed.

The program was finally over and the students were being congratulated by their relatives and teased by their friends. Dads would sneak outside for a quick smoke, the auctioneer started warming up and the teacher slumped in exhaustion against the wall.

The auction of boxes of candy got into full swing with spirited, competitive bidding and interesting little comments on the side. A daddy would slip his boy a couple of bucks to help the kid along. And there were blushes, giggles, laughter, teasing, squeals - oh, so much fun for these country people with the common ties of community and school - and not a whole lot of money, but shared memories of good times together.

The auction was over, the candy shared and all too soon it was time to go home. It was the best candy supper that had ever been held. Everybody said so - every year.

The proceeds from the auction and the sale of raffle tickets were used for school trips or baseball gloves, new bats or other playground equipment. Using those funds we once visited Hannibal, Mo., and the Tom Sawyer Cave; another time we went to the Mormon settlement in Nauvoo, Ill., and passed by the Iowa State Penitentiary in Fort Madison. The trip to view the pen must have made an impression - there were never any kids from Stringtown School who ever got into bad trouble.

Today, our kids have all kinds of ways to raise money for school projects. Why, in a single day I've been hit up to buy magazine subscriptions, school shirts, pizzas, expensive candy, cookies and knickknacks. There are all sorts of fund-raising 'thons: jogathons, walkathons, rockathons, as well as car washes and bake sales.

I can't believe, though, that there is as much enjoyment in those pursuits as there was for our candy supper held on a crisp fall night in a small one-room schoolhouse.

photo by Bob Nandell

Mama and Daddy - In sickness and in health.

My Dad's Mental Illness

I've seen many commercials and billboards which I've considered vulgar and tasteless, but I have never yet encountered one as offensive to me personally as a billboard I drive by regularly in Des Moines.

"Persons with Mental Illnesses Enrich All of Us!" claims the message on the billboard. In the background of the message are the names of greats in the arts and entertainment world - names like Ernest Hemingway, Sylvia Plath, Charles Dickens, Vincent Van Gogh and dozens of others. What these talented yet wretched souls had in common, aside from their works, was that all of them were mentally ill - usually manic depressive. Many committed suicide to escape their unhappiness or particular demons. The ad on the billboard is sponsored by the Alliance for the Mentally Ill.

Sadly, in the world of mental illness, my family and I were front row spectators. When I was in high school, mental illness hit close when one of my friends' dads was murdered by a neighbor who was mentally ill. Other families in our community were touched by tragedy and sudden, violent death from murder and suicide evolving from mental illness. Years earlier, when I was 10, I had experienced my own worries when my dad began acting strangely. He hadn't lived with us very long - I had been eight when he was brought home from a veterans hospital where he'd been for three years.

A generous and loving, jolly sort of man at first, as the months passed he became dour and unsmiling. He began talking to himself; sometimes he'd sit, grinding his teeth, talking to himself and raise his arm up in the air and leave it there. One day I upset him, and he turned me over his knee and began spanking me. He didn't stop. He just kept spanking, even after I'd cried all the tears which were in me and all the time he sort of stared off in the distance like he wasn't even aware of what he was doing.

It wasn't long after that when one afternoon he lurched out of his chair and backed my mother against the wall and began choking her. It's been 40 years since that happened, and I still clearly recall that time. My brother, who was eight, and I raced to help Mama, as we jumped up on Daddy's back, pounding at him and pulling on his overall suspenders, crying and screaming all the time, while Mama was trying to pry Daddy's hands loose.

As abruptly as it began, so too did it end with Daddy throwing Mama across the room where she crumpled and landed on her ankle, breaking it. He turned away as if nothing in the whole world had happened. I imagine, although I can't recall how the day ended exactly, that he went outside to do chores as usual. And it would have been natural for me to run across the way, while my brother looked after Mama, and tell my uncle and aunt what had happened.

I do know that my mother's uncle, Kenneth, who lived across the field, and a neighbor man, each of whom had watched daddy change and worsen, had a visit with my mom, later contacted the sheriff and soon Daddy was taken away to the state mental hospital in St. Joseph.

And that was the end of my brief experience of living in a two-parent family. A few years later, my dad came home a few times, but only on 30-day or 60-day furloughs or passes, and they were never particularly happy times.

It wasn't until after Daddy died in 1987 that Mama and I even talked much about his illness and what he had been like before he became sick. The conversation occurred one day when Mama said, "Your Daddy wasn't always like that, you know...." And yes, I had known that. Relatives had told stories of the man they knew, the hard-working, jolly, joking one. And in the two years he was well and living at home, I remember even now the love and affection he showed my mom, my brother and me.

Mama told me some of what had led up to his first hospitalization. And I've tried to imagine what it would have been like to be in her position then, a young farm wife in the late 1940s, early '50s, with two small children and a husband who was acting strange, and all the while being hundreds of miles away from family. Mental illness wasn't much discussed then, but it was right after the war and many GIs were having problems. My dad was in a GI young farmers' class and his instructor recognized something was going wrong with him, Mama told me.

I've tried to imagine what it was like to live with a man who was acting so odd and frightening, who slept on the floor with a shotgun and ate only cold, canned food because he thought someone was trying to poison him. And all the time having farm and household chores to tend to, along with two young children.

Then came the night, my mother told me, when she sent my brother and me to stay with neighbors. The sheriff came with other law officers, and had the electricity turned off so the house was dark. They shined headlights at the house, grabbed my dad and took him to the jail. He was later taken to the nearest veterans hospital.

The following years Daddy went through the most primitive, horrible, painful treatment, from electric shock to drugs.

The message on the Des Moines billboard about mental illness enriching us all was written, I imagine, by some young talent in an ad agency. I doubt, however, that it was created by anyone even remotely familiar with mental illness.

That "enriching experience" robbed my mother of the joys and even sorrows of a normal married life. Taking her marriage vows "in sickness and in health" seriously, she never sought to sever the ties that bound her and my dad together.

My brother, shortly after Daddy was taken away that early spring day of 1956, lost the ability to walk, and at the age of 10 crawled or had to be carried everywhere. In those days of polio, that was the big fear, that he had polio. Tests at the University of Iowa, including excruciating spinal taps, found that my brother did not have polio or any physical disorder. He was suffering from hysterical paralysis. Perhaps seeing Daddy try to harm our mom triggered his emotional responses.

And what has been the effect on me? It's hard to say - certainly it's never too far from my mind. Watching a person you love suffer from schizophrenia and paranoia, even when you're too young to have ever heard of the words - leaves a lasting impression.

Every life Daddy touched was somehow or other altered by the "enriching" experience of mental illness.

When I think of the word "enriching," I think of something joyful and wonderful or awe-inspiring. And while knowing my dad was a memorable experience, a frightening experience, a sad, tragic, painful, hurtful experience, I'm not sure I would ever call it an enriching experience.

Club Day

I don't belong to any clubs. I guess I'm not much of a joiner. For years I've been too lazy to fill out an application for a membership in the local American Legion Auxiliary to which I'm eligible to join as the sister of a Purple Heart former Marine, the daughter of a disabled veteran and the granddaughter of a decorated World War I veteran. But that is more or less an organization, and an organization differs greatly from a regular club. No, the type of club to which I'm referring is one like my mom's when I was a kid: An extension club. An extension club was one part educational, but mostly social and for enjoyment. Extension clubs were a part of the Extension Service which came out of the state university, as I understood it.

Our rural neighborhood was known as Stringtown. Where that name came from, I don't know. There was no town, only a one-room school and a small country church. But my mom's club was known as the Stringtown Extension Club. All the neighbor ladies met every two weeks for an all-day club session in the home of a member.

The hostess would have a project on hand on which the other members pitched in. Usually the project was a quilt. The children of the hostess would hope the ladies were fast quilters. Otherwise, most of the following weeks would be spent dodging a quilt in frames which took up most of the floor space of the living room. And woe be unto the young innocent who threw an armload of books onto a quilt-in-progress.

Other projects included picking out nutmeats. A lady's family could be kept busy for weeks before a club meeting just picking up and cracking dish pans and buckets full of hickory nuts and walnuts. Or club members might help tear up, sew and roll up into big balls all the rags and worn-out clothing for the making of rag rugs. Or maybe the hostess needed a couple of rooms wallpapered. The ladies would arrive at the club meeting armed with brushes, rollers and ladders. Once, my mom had her friends come in their old work clothes or wearing their husbands' overalls or jeans, and they roofed our cow shed with corrugated metal roofing. That was a sight to behold coming home from school, believe me.

And the meals on club day! None of this cheese-and-crackers, nuts-and-mints stuff. No sir, we're talking some heavy-duty, substantial food. A country neighborhood covered-dish dinner with stewed hen and noodles, mounds of potatoes, casseroles, vegetables, salads, pies, cakes, and relishes. New recipes were proudly introduced, copied down and exchanged. Husbands of the members would show up as noontime neared, coming in from their field work. They would wash up, and in this time 15 or 20 years before women's liberation was ever discussed, the women would wait until their menfolk were finished filling their plates before beginning themselves. Lucky was the family of the hostess because when the kids came home from school, there were piles of leftovers!

Following the meal and after the dishes were washed, the regular meeting would take place with the roll call, a Bible reading, and since it was an

Extension club, they'd have a lesson on something like how to get rid of squash bugs or ease in the sleeve of a homemade dress. Then as the ladies quilted and visited with one another across the quilt, bingo was usually played. My mom still has evidence of numerous bingo games around the house in the guise of candy dishes, vases, head scarves and doilies she won as prizes.

There are very few Extension clubs left that I know of, and those are anemic compared to when my mom's club was in full swing.

Oh yes, I can remember club day when the driveway was full of cars and pickups and you knew that there, in that house, was the home of someone whose relative had just died, or a lady who was having a club meeting. And if it were a Thursday in the Stringtown neighborhood, you knew it was club.

'Cause nobody dared die on club day.

Becoming Educated Without A Degree

The words took me by surprise.

"Boy, Mom," said my daughter Jenny, who was 12 at the time, "You sure know a lot for never going to college."

I'd been helping her with her homework. We'd been discussing Europe, something in geography, and I'd told her of the countries that no longer are countries, mixing a little bit of politics, some history and geography, trying to make it sound real and interesting.

It doesn't take a college degree to be interested in the world around us and to read newspapers, books and other sources to learn about world events. But that's apparently surprising to some, including my daughter.

That's something I've run in to every now and then, a subtle air of snobbery, even elitism, among many of those with a college degree or two or three.

"Where did you get your journalism degree?" I'm asked. I haven't got one, I answer. "Well, where did you go to school?" I went to a small high school in Missouri, I respond. "No, no, where did you go to college?" I didn't, I answer, and with my typical thin skin, begin to feel as if I should apologize and that I'm being viewed as slightly unintelligent, probably backward, almost certainly an intellectual inferior.

These days going on to college after high school graduation is taken for granted by our youngsters. It is considered an extension of one's education as naturally as high school follows grade school and junior high.

I sometimes feel that to merely have a high school diploma, once considered quite an achievement and something to be coveted and treasured, is to be viewed as a person who's less than whole, perhaps even a bit slow or semiliterate on top of that.

When I was a teenager planning my future - well, I didn't plan my future, really. And our high school guidance counselor - one of those omnipotent beings who counsel students on careers, grades, furthering education, acne, prom dates and remind parents ominously about Financial Aid Forms and ACT test scores - didn't direct my future. Our counselor was an older woman who wore her hair in finger waves, had jowls, and a bad overbite - sort of resembling pictures I'd seen of Eleanor Roosevelt - and always had spit forming at the corners of her mouth; it was fascinating to watch, really. She wore Red Cross shoes and carried a stop watch to time our aptitude tests. She also showed college recruiters the location of the high school cafeteria where we met to listen to their pitches, or used the meeting as an excuse to get out of class - usually the latter. As far as I know our counselor never influenced anyone's future one way or the other. Except that nobody became a guidance counselor.

My plan after school was to get married. But since my sweetheart's parents and my mom didn't share that view, the next thing was to find a job. There was no work in my home town, so that meant going to the city, Des Moines or Kansas City. Des Moines was closer.

College had never even been a consideration. In the first place, we couldn't afford it. And in the second place, I had no particular call to be a teacher or a nurse - those being the two professions considered worthwhile for the college-bound female.

I'd had a lot of secretarial-type courses in school. It would be my destiny to be an office worker. Newspaper work wasn't even considered. Nobody from Unionville, Mo., did that except for the Stuckey family who'd had the local paper forever. Writing wasn't a vocation. Being a writer, everyone knows, is not REALLY a job.

No, my high school diploma had the dust of 15 years on it when I first entered the field of newspaper work - and then strictly by happenstance.

But over those years I took a deep interest in news. And I also love to read. Anything. Newspapers, news magazines, novels, spy stories, romances, historical novels, biographies - anything. Except for car owner's manuals, warranties, and the instructions for any gadget or appliance.

I've always regretted I never paid much attention to Mrs.Magee's world history class in high school. But in 10th grade, which is when it was offered when I was a kid, there were more important things to consider such as boys, clothes, my flat chest and pimples.

World wars, border clashes, Egyptian tombs, Cro-Magnon man, Chinese dynasties, the Monroe Doctrine , the genealogies and intrigues of European royalty weren't that important.

The last time I paid close attention to geography was probably in sixth grade. Later on my sources were Time Magazine and The Des Moines Register, and by that time the names of countries and their borders were completely different. When's the last time anyone ever heard of the Belgium Congo or French Indo-China?

As for writing, I learned a love for verbs, fancy turns of phrases, nice-sounding adjectives and adventurous adverbs from teachers I had in a one-room country school in Missouri. My love of reading and learning to finely craft a descriptive sentence came at the hands of country school teachers who more likely than not possessed teaching certificates instead of college degrees. Their love of the profession, their respect for kids' minds, and their expectations that we use those minds, did as much for me as did the degreed men and women later on in high school.

Diagramming sentences, conjugating verbs, writing book reports - those were the preparations that went into making me a writer. That and the weekly letters home to my mom, my grandparents and my brother in the Marines overseas.

"Where did you learn to write?" my daughter asked me."

"Well, honey, I guess I didn't really *learn* to write," I answered. "Writing is one of those things that just sort of comes with a person, I guess. The same thing, probably, that made me right-handed and brown-eyed."

That answer appeared to satisfy her.

Grandpa And The Crawdads

I read a wire service story in the paper the other day. The story was about the grief and destruction that crawdads are causing in southern states, particularly Texas, with the crawdad's mud chimney-type homes in the ground. The little crawdad houses are tearing up pastures and ruining farm implements. Texans are wondering what they're going to do about the little critters.

I've got a story about how one man dealt with crawdads.

Today, you'll learn of one of my more colorful relatives, my mom's late father, my grandpa, Ozem Lachem Kingston, former soldier, coal miner, farmer, bootlegger, ladies' man and regular man-about-town. He was a combination of Jesse James, John Wayne and Don Juan. Incidentally, he hated crawdads.

I don't remember meeting Grandpa until I was about 12. I suppose it was when he brought his new wife to meet the family. Several years passed and I married and started my own family. Grandpa's wife died, and my mom decided that we'd drive to Kansas, just she and I and my six-month-old son, to visit Grandpa. That 1967 trip was the beginning of an annual summer pilgrimage of visiting Grandpa. And it was during those visits that I came to know him.

Grandpa lived in a dusty, nearly forgotten town in southeastern Kansas - Mulberry, Kan.

It was probably a booming town in the late 1800s, but when we visited there it boasted only a post office, gas station, a tavern, grocery store and 97 widow ladies. (My grandpa had them counted and listed in his mind in order of age, appearance, assets and appetites.)

My grandpa wasn't much of a housekeeper so the first couple of days of our yearly visit was spent with Saniflush, Mr. Clean, Clorox, brooms and mops. "Bless you girls' hearts," our old charmer would say, "You sure know how to take care of your poor ol' daddy."

Grandpa had a Bad Stomach brought on, he claimed, by fighting "them damn Germans" in World War I, and ex-wives for the next 50 years. His former wives numbered four or five until the year, because of a slip of his tongue, Mama and I wormed out of him that he had, in fact, gotten married again since we'd last seen him. It had lasted two weeks. She had been younger than I, his granddaughter, and had, Grandpa claimed, liked to read in bed which made her uh...incompatible with my grandpa who was only in his 70s, still a young man with a robust nature....

Grandpa's ulcers were the cause of confrontations between his daughter and himself. Since regular food upset his stomach, he stuck to egg nogs and his own concoction of ice cream, eggs, and about half a quart of Jack Daniels, followed by bottles of beer to wash it down. To keep his insides working properly, he also drank Dr. Pepper, which he believed was made of carbonated prune juice. If he wanted a regular meal, he would fry pork steak and make milk gravy from the drippings. He'd eat the gravy and give the pork steak to his beloved cats. And that is where he and my mom really locked horns. Not over his poor housekeeping or his ex-wives, but over feeding good pork steak to cats. Because he did love his cats. Nearly as much as he hated crawdads.

Crawdads had invaded Grandpa's yard one summer and if he hadn't already had a Bad Stomach, those crawdads would've given him one. He stomped in and destroyed their mud huts in the evening, but they'd be back by the next morning. He couldn't even flood them out with the water hose.

He'd fought Germans in France, had trouble with liquor law-enforcement in the dry state of Oklahoma; he had run-ins with angry former spouses and in-laws. And he had triumphed. But the crawdads were wearing Grandpa down.

If they were coming up through his lawn, he reasoned, he'd make it so the little *&%$#@ couldn't. He had tons and tons of fine gravel trucked in and spread on his once-green lawn. And that fixed the crawdads! For a while.

There were still a few tenacious crawdads that managed to burrow up and those few were enough to keep Grandpa busy and entertained. Some senior citizens may travel or play bingo for recreation. My grandpa killed crawdads. (When he wasn't busy keeping track of the widow ladies.)

He had a supply of carbide, which he brought into his arsenal to be used against the crawdads. Carbide is a granular substance used by miners in pit lamps - when dampened, it gives off a noxious gas and really stinks.

I can see him yet in his folding chair out in the yard with a pitcher of water, a can of carbide and his cup of eggnog - the cats wrapping themselves around his legs - as he relentlessly pursued the crawdads by pouring carbide down their holes, followed by a stream of water. "Come on out of there, you little ***&^%$#. I'll getcha yet, you #$%^&*!" he'd crow in glee.

And in the evening after a hard day of fighting crawdads and in between innings of his favorite St. Louis Cardinals ballgames, Grandpa would tell me tales of World War I battles -he was a decorated veteran with a Purple Heart -and of Paris and some of the less reputable business establishments there; of his relationship with his second (or maybe it was his third) wife's cousin, a guy by the same of Pretty Boy Floyd. He startled me into speechlessness one time by being astonished that any granddaughter of his would actually believe that a man had walked on the moon. "Why them guys walked on a mesa down in Arizona, and had people thinking they were on the moon! Why, they even fooled that old bastard, Cronkite!"

That rascally grandpa of mine was something else.

When I was growing up and would do or say something ornery or even naughty, as I sometimes did, people who had known my grandpa would say to my mom, "That girl of yours has a lot of Ozem Kingston in her." And then they'd start smiling and chuckling.

And that's the way it is today. When we think of or reminisce about Grandpa, we inevitably start smiling at the memories, and finally laughing at some of the outrageous things he said and did.

Aren't fond memories one of the best legacies we can receive from those we love?

The Passing Of A Country Doctor

"They buried Dr. Mac this week," my mom told me as we visited at her kitchen table.

I was sorry to hear that. Dr. McDonald, or Dr. Mac as he was always called, had played a significant part in the lives of a rural Missouri family skirting the edge of poverty.

Dr. Mac was our family doctor for - well, forever, it seemed. On a warm September day in 1945 Dr. Mac delivered a bouncing baby girl to Juanita and Max Pickett; the new daddy was stationed at Camp Roberts, Calif., and would receive the news via a telegram which still rests in a box of family keepsakes. The new mother lived with her parents while awaiting the return of her husband from the Army.

That was the beginning of my relationship with Dr. Mac. And though we didn't visit the doctor's office often, I always knew him with his silvery blond hair, rimless glasses and the gold crowns on his teeth gleaming when he smiled.

During the mass inoculations of the newly-discovered polio vaccine in the 1950s, I could always count on seeing Dr. Mac somewhere around when hundreds of youngsters came to the county courthouse to be vaccinated against the frightening ever-present threat of polio. "D'ya want to live in an iron lung or be crippled and wear braces the rest of your life?" many a parent asked children who were reluctant to receive the painful inoculation.

Five years after he delivered me, Dr. Mac was removing my tonsils. Of that episode I remember being terribly sick because of the ether anesthesia. I also recall being served ice cream and Jello while I was laying in a narrow hospital bed missing my mama and wanting to go home.

It was a stormy, rainy night in April, 1957, when my mom became worried enough to call Dr. Mac. I had been sick with a sideache and nausea the whole rainy day. I was curled up on the living room sofa with a washpan on the floor beside me when Dr. Mac carrying his little black bag came in the door on a gust of wind and rain. He checked my temperature, asked Mama some questions and then said, "I reckon we'll have to take this girl to the hospital."

I was 11 years old - a big girl, I thought - but I remember to this day the reassuring feel of Dr. Mac's arms coming around me as he effortlessly lifted me up and carried me up our long, muddy lane to his car to take me to the hospital. I recall laying on a long, flat table, looking up at a big bright light with Dr. Mac peering down at me with his kind eyes peeking from above the surgical mask and the familiar glasses glinting in the light. "Now you be a big girl," he said, "This'll be over real soon and you'll feel a lot better. Now I'm going to put this over your face and...."

...And I woke up later in a different room not feeling real good, but with no appendix remaining to give me trouble.

A few years later it would be my younger brother, Mike, critically ill with a ruptured appendix who Dr. Mac would care for. My poor, worried mom was comforted when he put his arm around her shoulders and patted her arm gently as he told her everything would be okay. "....And don't you worry about the bill," he told her in this day and age before Medicaid, "We'll work something out," he said to the woman who supported her family with what could be produced on a 19-acre farm and a measly pittance of a check from the Veterans Administration. My kid-ears picked all this up as Mama related it to my grandma later.

Time passed. A hot summer Sunday after church found my mom laying on the sofa in just her slip to rest a while, when she tried to get up, put on her old clothes and fix dinner. As she raised up on her elbow, she got an awful look on her face and let out a scream, falling back on the sofa whimpering. My brother and I - we were probably 13 and 11 - were scared to death, and Mama was crying. She never cried! I ran across the field to get my Uncle Kenneth, who called the doctor. Good Dr. Mac soon arrived with his little black bag, and diagnosed a "bad back." He soothed Mama and got her straightened up a little with a jury-rigged back-brace, and then turned to us kids easing our fears that she wasn't dying; she'd just hurt her back a little and we'd have to be good kids and help her as much as we could.

It was school homecoming night and I was 16 when next I remember needing the services of Dr. Mac. I was in a car that went off a gravel road. Actually, the '52 Ford kinda rolled over four or five times in a big ditch, hit a culvert, flipped up in the air and end-over-ended three or four more times. I told my mom later only that the car had gone in the ditch when it hit loose gravel. It would be several years before she found out the whole truth.

I was with my cousin Sue and her face was cut up quite a bit; her boyfriend, Bill, now her husband of many years - was banged around, too. My nose had hit an immovable object and the roof of the car had come down and hit me smack on top of the head giving me an awful headache. My knees had banged into the dash and with everyone bleeding so much I was sort of scared. The Highway Patrol came, as well as the sheriff. He took us to the doctor's office, and of course it would be Dr. Mac. "What's your mother going to say about this?" he asked as he wiped the blood from my face and packed gauze stuff up my nose while I winced and cried a little more.

"Oh please, Dr. Mac," I pleaded, "Don't tell her. Please?"

"Now don't start crying again," he said as he patted my shoulder, "You're a big girl now, but you really shouldn't do things that'll worry your mother, you know."

Following news of his death, my hometown newspaper printed the story under the headline, "Community mourns loss of Dr. Mac."

The community is larger, I guess, than the headline implied.

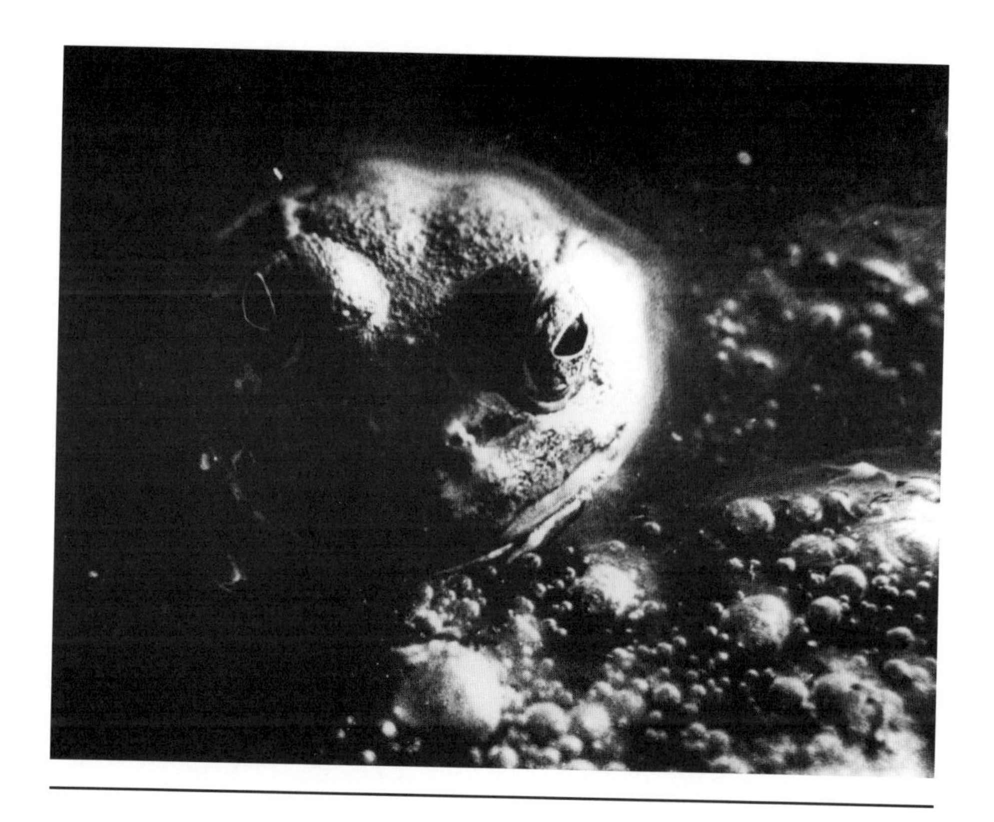

Frogs In Tornado Alley

I doubt if there's anything quite as nice as spring in the Midwest.

Show me something prettier than a spring morning with a clear blue sky and the green tinge of new grass. Listen to the sounds of meadowlarks and robins; or the neighbor's tractor already out in the field; or to new lambs and calves bleating for their mamas. Hear the gurgle of water flowing into a nearby stream, or the remnants of a flock of geese flying north.

Give me the smells of emerging tree buds, of spring flowers, of freshly turned Mother Earth. I revel in the dusty, earthy smell of the air after a rainfall.

The one serpent in this spring Eden is that besides being a time of rebirth and renewal, it's also a time for tornadoes.

Snakes and tornadoes, both similar in appearance, both sneaky; each is terrifying.

When I was a young girl living in Missouri, we rarely heard of tornadoes so I was never really afraid of them. They always seemed to occur in Texas or Oklahoma or Kansas.

Later, after I was married and living in Des Moines, I never worried much about tornadoes. I had read or heard somewhere that a tornado will never strike where two rivers join. And while meteorologists may scoff at this old wives' tale, it nevertheless gave me quite a bit of reassurance.

Several years ago we moved 40 miles south of Des Moines to the foothills of Warren County. We moved in April at the very beginning of tornado season.

I'll never forget that spring. Ever.

We lived in a mobile home then. For the first few weeks we didn't have electricity, water or the telephone connected. The trailer hadn't been leveled out yet, much less tied down as it was supposed to be.

Bob worked nights in Des Moines. We had only two sons, a three-year-old, a one-year-old and another on the way. We didn't know a soul.

It's one thing to dream of moving to the country. It's quite another to be pregnant and alone with two little boys and no family or friends nearby, listening to a static-filled transistor radio broadcasting tornado warnings for southern Warren County on a dark, windy, spooky night.

I still remember those long nights with the smells of rain, mud and kerosene lamps; the sounds of thunder, wind, hail and tree branches hitting the side of the trailer. I can still recall the sight of lightning illuminating the whole barren, muddy landscape.

I mentally blessed the person who had decades earlier planted the cedar tree windbreak just west of the trailer. Imagine me ever thinking those cedar trees were brown and ugly and of planning someday to have them bulldozed away! They still stand today, those lovely cedar trees, affectionately cared for by our family.

The one thing that kept me from coming unglued during those lonely and terrifying nights was frogs.

Yes, that's right. Frogs.

During the storming and blowing and broadcast tornado warnings, I would warily open the door and peer out, fully expecting to see or hear a twister come down to snatch me and my babies away. The sound that came to my ears, though, was the sound of frogs croaking their welcome spring chorus.

For some reason I felt that if anything awful were going to happen, the frogs wouldn't croak. And as long as I could still hear them, then things would be OK.

Today we live in a house with a snug and safe basement. We have a scanner with a weather monitor to warn us when severe weather is approaching.

But the thing that makes me feel safe and secure during tornado season is the same as it was all those years ago, the barnyard croakers - our frogs.

Bless their little green souls.

Good Old Golden Rule Days

Cries of teen-age indignation are being heard in many homes of high school students these days. It seems that there is a crackdown on discipline, behavior and dress codes coming on. No longer are couples allowed to neck or make out in school hallways. T-shirts and other items of apparel bearing messages that are improper or advertising alcohol or tobacco are not allowed. Shorts, crop-tops and halter tops are forbidden for girls in seventh grade and over. Swearing at, mouthing back or threatening teachers and other school personnel, I understand, is being frowned on. Food fights are declining in cafeterias.

I have three words to respond to this reported crackdown.

It's about time.

I listen to complaints about current school policy and I smile. How great, I think, now maybe some of these mouthy monsters will learn something besides anarchy.

I don't know when education's lax standards came about or when I even noticed it. Perhaps it was an off-shoot of the hippie-flower-child-do-your-own-thing, I'm OK, You're OK school of thought. Perhaps it was when the government started nosing in with its entitlement programs, or when American Civil Liberties Union attorneys started filing lawsuits against schools, and parents brought in their own lawyers. I do know I noticed a lack of respect for authority probably about the time my boys entered junior high, if not before, when I began hearing of 10-year-olds swearing at teachers; 13-year-olds being suspended for abusive behavior; thousands of dollars in damage done annually to school property by vandals - - just a general lack of respect for other people or property or authority figures. The widespread use of really foul language also filtered in and it was nothing to walk down the hall of the elementary school and hear THAT word several times from boys as well as girls, along with several other choice expletives which would curl the hair of a truck driver, or even a newspaper columnist.

And that's in a comparatively small rural school district. Can you imagine what it would be like in a city? My cousin-the-school-superintendent, in a large city in Missouri, has a metal detector by the door to his office and often has to frisk students for weapons.

I tell these stories to my own sons and then begin a sentence which causes them to roll their eyes dramatically and take a deep breath. The words?

WHEN I WAS A KID:

Students didn't have rights. Kids didn't have rights and everyone was happy - except maybe the habitual trouble-makers and everyone knew they'd end up no-account anyway. Teachers stood right next to God, and on His other side were the principal and superintendent.

Dress codes? Certainly. No female was allowed to wear shorts or slacks in school. They could be worn while decorating the gym for prom or when getting ready to leave on a class skating party. Why, the subject wasn't even thought of or discussed. Some girls, if they had to walk a distance or stand quite a while in cold weather awaiting the school bus, might wear slacks under their skirts, but most girls would rather freeze than be uncool or be seen wearing slacks under a skirt like they were pantaloons.

Also guys could not have whiskers, sideburns or even longish hair. But who would want to besides hoods or a beatnik - like some really squirrelly guy playing bongo drums on the Ed Sullivan Show.

Behavior? No running or bumping in halls; no slamming or kicking lockers; do not go up the down stairs, nor down the up stairs. When couples met during class breaks, two pairs of hands had to be in plain sight. Ball bearings being stealthily rolled across the length of study hall was guaranteed to draw snickers but generally was frowned on, as was anointing hot water pipes with skunk oil. Unruly behavior on the bus? You were kicked off and made to walk - no hearing, either, except the one you'd receive from your folks.

Respect for most teachers, yes, except the foolish few who tried to fit in with us - be one of us. For school administrators, yes. They ran a tight ship, which could be a little risky at times. I remember one Saturday night when a boy's dad got a little drunk and showed up at the principal's home with a squirrel gun. He was mad because his kid had gotten into trouble at school. No one got shot, but the kid was pretty embarrassed on Monday morning.

And back before school superintendents became enmeshed in budgets, civil suits, the feds and entitlement programs, state legislatures, seminars and forums, we had our superintendent, Mr. Wickless, alias god with a small g.

He seemed to be everywhere. He had a gruff, deep voice - one like Noah might've heard or Moses from the burning bush. He was a gray-haired giant of a man and you would think from the way he acted most students were non-persons to him. That is, until he noticed your existence and smiled at you or patted you on the back; or if, God forbid, you had been unruly, broken the rules, attracted his notice and been hauled by the shirt collar into his office. There, you would be chewed out, lectured on proper behavior and would either have apologized or said good-bye and perhaps have been suspended or expelled.

And yet with what some would view as a rigid environment and strict discipline, my high school years evoke the fondest memories and were the best times. Discipline? Yes. Authority? Yes. But also a solid education when we were expected to amount to something, respect, values, good times, laughter and long-lasting friendships.

It saddens me to think that even my kids speak about those times as "the good old days."

Sunday Morning Reverie

I sat in church one Sunday morning. It was during that time of the morning worship service after the offering plate has been passed and just before the preacher has gotten warmed up good; that time when the congregation is getting settled into seats, ready for the sermon and trying not to think of chores waiting at home or what to fix for dinner; that time when little kids get their last restless wiggles in, throats are cleared and noses are blown one last time - and then the peaceful, soul-soothing silence of a Sunday morning prayer time.

It was during this time as my eyes ranged up our pew, checking to see if my kids' heads were all properly bowed, that my eyes encountered a pair of hands resting between denim-clad knees. They were large hands, hands that I hadn't really looked closely at for quite a long time. They were the hands of a young man - the hands of my son.

Why he's almost a man, I thought to myself. For such a long time, 17 years in fact, he's been my oldest son, but still, always a little boy to me.

Last week he was 16 years old. But he's had a birthday since then and somehow or other, 17 seems much older.

I stared at the hands and in those few moments of Sunday morning silence, my mind ranged over 17 years in the life of a boy.

I remembered those hands, those fingers, when they were so tiny, nearly match-stick size, and they waved around in the air, finally finding and grasping my finger. I remember Bob and me counting fingers and toes on a two-hour-old first baby when we were almost afraid to touch him, afraid we'd damage something in our first-time-parents' awe and clumsiness.

That thumb was once a cherished friend. It kept this son of mine company as he slept in his crib, and later alone in a big bed as a new baby brother displaced him. That thumb was grudgingly relinquished as a best friend when he was getting ready to enter kindergarten, after he had become a "big boy" who was too old to suck his thumb.

Those large, man-sized hands were once small and trusting. One hand was placed in my hand as I walked him to the school bus on his first day of school, and I was able to smile encouragingly even though my heart was aching for him on his new venture.

I guided that hand as it laboriously practiced printing the letters M-I-K-E, and we were so proud of what that hand could do. I watched that hand and those fingers as a daddy patiently taught his son the important things in a boy's life - like how to put a worm on a fishhook so it wouldn't drop off, or how to hold a hammer and pound in a nail, or the proper way to hold a ball bat.

As I sat in church on that Sunday morning while sleet fell outside and we were warm and snug inside, my mind traveled on and on as I stared at the young man's hands.

I remember when those hands were just 10 years old and getting acquainted with a new baby sister. Those hands had more confidence in holding a five-day-old infant than I could accept with any peace of mind. "I can hold her by myself, Mom! See? Yes, I'm holding the back of her head good. Boy, she's awful little and so cute! Look, she's smiling at me!" And I remembered the other babies he'd held, like his two brothers, one when he was two and a-half, and again when he was an experienced baby handler of four. And then his joy in two baby sisters. Those hands always enjoyed holding babies, making a lie of the rule that boys don't like babies and aren't good with them.

I was so proud of those little-boy hands as they carried the flag when he marched with his Cub Scout pack in the local Old Settlers parade during the U.S. Bicentennial year, and later as he recited from memory and with no prompting the Gettysburg Address while his hands nervously gripped the microphone. Those hands grew rapidly over the next few years and I casually watched as they built model cars and planes. Later, they scraped and cleaned the hooves of his horse. Along the way they helped mom stem strawberries and pick peas; they picked up little sisters as they toddled and fell; swatted brothers and threw snowballs. They grew rough and callused from helping bale hay and working as a farm hand for the neighbor.

Last year the hands came home blood covered from a car wreck. I washed and bandaged the cuts and slashes, thanked God I still had my son, and swore I'd never yell at him again, which of course I did as soon as I stopped shaking and he got some color back in his face.

Now those hands, those man-sized hands, help me over icy patches and open the door for me. They go around my shoulders when he's feeling extra sweet or wants something. They have been seen to slip around my waist when he says to a friend, "I'd like you to meet my mom!" And it's times like those I have trouble keeping the happy, mother-pride tears from my eyes.

All of these thoughts coursed through my mind as I looked at those hands in the few moments before the preacher's sermon. It was with force of will that I tried to concentrate on the sermon. It was something from Psalms about "...bearing force precious seed and rejoicing..."

Somehow it seem quite appropriate as a companion to my thoughts.

photo by Bob Nandell

Heirloom Hankies

Lace-Edged Hankies

"What's this?" my daughter asked as we were sorting through a box of no-longer-used-but-too-nice-to-throw-away stuff.

When I saw what she was holding up, I felt like a throwback to Victorian days as I stared at the relic in her hand.

"Why, that's a hanky," I told her.

Hankies. How long had it been since I'd even thought of them? This particular handkerchief was white with red hearts, and I'd gotten it in a valentine's card when I was in grade school.

That's something hankies were good for - modest gifts to be enclosed in a pretty card - or for an even fancier gift - a whole box of handkerchiefs in a cellophane-topped container.

All ladies, young and otherwise, had hankies up until a few years ago. And I can't help but think the world was a better and saner place for their presence and use.

Tissues weren't used by anyone much. I remember the one mama's boy who was in fifth grade and used lavender-colored Kleenex. I've never forgotten that. To this day, there's a large question mark in my mind when I think of him.

Hankies were the most useful accessories ever invented. Aside from using them for that which they were intended - wiping and blowing one's nose - they had many other uses.

They were absolutely essential to have at weddings and funerals to be used to wipe damp eyes or at least act like you might need to wipe away some tears.

Hankies were wash cloths for mothers. Licked, they could be used to give one those vigorous "spit baths" mothers are so good at when taking chocolate or grime off the face of a small child. Or if a water fountain or other water source was handy, I've known mothers who could practically bathe a kid with a wetted-down handkerchief.

Once there was a time before a little girl ever had her own purse (formerly called a pocketbook) or billfold, she had a pretty hanky of her own. And in the corner of the hanky could be tied her Sunday school offering money or her dime allowance.

Ladies carried handkerchiefs under wristwatch bands, stuck up sleeves, stuffed down into the cleavage of large, pendulous bosoms, clutched in a dainty fist or, if it were a particularly pretty handkerchief, worn in a pocket with the edging showing or tucked in the side pocket of a purse with the edging gracefully draped.

And the edgings, oh, the edgings! There was a time when all county fairs had entries for handkerchief edgings made of tatting or crochet-work. New or different edging instructions were shared with all the zeal of today's zucchini recipe exchanges. My mom and grandma were very good edging-makers. They made it by the yard, I swear, in plain colors and variegated, simple or fancy wide-ruffled edging, or just a thin little piece of trim attached to the linen square. Hankies were gifts for relatives, secret pals at club meetings, grab bags, get-well or thank-you gifts.

I can remember rummaging through my grandma's purse during church and getting out her pretty never-used hanky - my favorite one was red with black and red crocheted edging. It always smelled of her perfume and the Clove chewing gum she always carried with her. I'd sit and play with the crocheted edging, fanning it out, crimping, counting stitches - anything to while away time until the sermon was over.

Later on, after I was in high school, only a complete drip - those destined to be old maids or worse - would have been caught dead with a handkerchief. Having one's own box of Kleenex, rather than wads of the stuff stuck in a purse, was very cool. But if I needed a gift to give to a favorite teacher, I'd turn to my mom or grandma and cadge a pretty crochet-trimmed hanky.

Today, hankies are relegated to the bottom dresser drawer or box of keepsakes. The only handkerchiefs we have are the big red or blue bandannas that I use to hold my hair back.

Pretty hankies, a certain sign of gentility and civilized demeanor in another era, are regarded as relics today.

I thought of all these things as I tried to explain to my daughter the many and varied uses of handkerchiefs.

I must have done a good job because she was satisfied and had another story about the old days and turned once again to rummaging. I moved to leave only to be asked another question as she held up more items. "Where did you wear these?" she asked.

"Oh gosh, those are my good white gloves ..."

Hometown Visits

Hometowns are great. Everybody should have one.

A July Fourth weekend found our family traveling to my hometown in Missouri.

Our children live in a community here in Iowa where they are known by neighbors, friends and school classmates. But we have no family members living in the community except those found in our house. Where my children's friends have uncles, aunts, cousins, in-laws and grandparents nearby - our kids have no relatives living close.

The kids find, though, what it's like to have extended family members when they visit my hometown with me. And that was the case during the July Fourth holiday visit with my mom when the boys paid a visit to the town square checking to see if there was any action in town, or better yet, any young ladies.

Usually there are dozens of young people parked around the town square in the evening as they congregate in their cars or 4-wheel drive pickups - gun racks in the back windows and radios blasting out rock music. It's a favorite pasttime, and about the only one left for them since the theaters closed.

Our boys were noticed as strangers in town by their fellow teens on the square. "Who're you here visitin'?" asked one of the young cowboys.

"We're here from Iowa visiting our grandma - maybe you know her, Juanita Pickett?" said my son. "Oh sure, I know her," said the kid, "She delivered me." That bit of news astounded my sons both at the smallness of the world and the fact that their Grandma Pickett, a nurse for many years, had delivered the young man when the doctor was late getting to the hospital.

Another time during the weekend of family discoveries as two of our teen-aged sons were walking down the sidewalk next to the main drag - not only is it known as Main Street, but it's also U.S. Highway 136 - they noticed a carload of nice-looking teenage girls. One remark led to another until the startling discovery was made when they got a closer look at the driver - she looked familiar. "Hey, it's our cousin!" the boys exclaimed as they recognized the 19-year-old girl seen only at family reunions. A respite from the boredom of "Mom's hometown," followed with conversation between Missouri young ladies and Iowa boys. Later, as the boys continued their stroll, a horn sounded. They looked up at a pickup - another cousin had recognized them. "Now what's his name - you know, he's been at the family reunion and has the droopy mustache - Joe Dean - yeah, that's who it was, and later on we saw his boys. What are they to us? Fourth or fifth cousins?"

"This is really neat," they reported on their return to their grandma's place. "I didn't know we had this many cousins."

I grew up around little but family in the hills of Missouri. My great-grandfather lived right across the field from us in the place where my grandmother and her brothers and sisters were raised; the place where my daddy met Mama as he was boarding in my great-grandparents' home; the house that held so many memories for so many generations - the site of many family reunions.

My mom is an only child. My grandma isn't, and 14 babies were born in that old yellow, two-story house of my great-grandparents, and those who survived were the great-aunts and uncles who provided plenty of second cousins, and most of them lived not far away. In fact, many of my second cousins seem as close as brothers and sisters, it seems. And their kids and my kids - and here the blood is beginning to thin considerably, making my kids and their kin fourth - sometimes fifth and sixth cousins, are nearly strangers to one another.

At family gatherings they look warily at each other for a short while only - remaining strangers only briefly. They've heard the same family stories, passed from one generation to another - they've seen the same age-old family photographs that my brother and I looked at when we were little - that my mom also looked at or posed for, as well as our grandma. Occasionally a genetic time bomb will appear in the guise of a growing youngster with some of the characteristics or personality traits of a long-remembered common ancestor.

Hometowns are wonderful places to return to, a place to renew the ties that bind - to appreciate anew the changelessness of things.

The United States Mail

When I was a kid, one of my favorite times of the day was when the mailman went past. There was nearly always something left for us and it could be a race sometimes to see who would be the first to reach the mailbox, my brother or me.

Since I was two years older and had longer legs, it was usually me. That is, until his hormones kicked in and a sudden growth spurt during his 13th summer found him shooting past me, allowing him to not only outrun me, but to become stronger and tougher. I was no longer able to whip him in our fights.

I imagine there were a few times when our mail carrier intervened in our fights as he attempted to hand one of us the mail while we scrapped over it.

In our mail were letters from relatives and friends. Occasionally our mom would call us in to listen as she read letters to us. My brother and I made a rapt audience as she would silently read a few lines to herself, then "....oh, and listen to this..." and we would be treated to more comments from the letter-writer mingled with those from our mother.

Newspapers, too, came to our home. The Unionville Republican, the local weekly, as well as another one, The Capper's Weekly, which was published in Kansas and contained all sorts of world and national news, as well as recipes, a serial story, and letters from ladies telling how they'd triumphed or dealt with particular problems or sharing household tips. Kind of like a rural Ann Landers and Heloise, all rolled into one.

Seed catalogs and wish books like Sears, Spurgeons and National Bellas Hess catalogs were regular visitors in our home.

I sold seeds for the Henry Field Seed Company for a couple of years when I was in grade school. The orders, as well as my special prizes for selling the seeds, came in the mail. Their arrivals were always exciting.

Later when I was in high school, I received letters from my boyfriend, and woe be unto the person who touched those letters with the S.W.A.K. printed in large letters on the back of the envelope, telling the whole world, including the mail carrier, that the letter had been "sealed with a kiss." The mail carrier would always gently tease me about the letters I received.

My heart would be going pitty-pat as I hurried off to a private spot to read the letter. Certain juicy portions of the letter would be shared with my cousin, Sue, who lived next to us. She and I would gasp and giggle and become silly over the letters which, on reflection, were probably juvenile, but nevertheless were quite romantic in the eyes of a 16-year-old.

And more letters were sent out from our home to friends and relatives in this time - and it doesn't seem all that long ago - before direct-dialing and long-distance calls made letter-writing virtually a folk craft, something akin to spinning and weaving.

Well, I'm no longer a grade school kid, nor a lovesick high school junior, but the arrival of the mailman is no less a treat today than it was back then.

Our family's mailman, like the one I knew as a kid, was practically like another member of our family. He settled disputes between brothers and sisters over who was going to be handed the mail. He handed out sticks of gum and passed the time of day with youngsters who could just barely see over the car door into the window as he delivered the mail to our country mailbox.

I remember the first time I met our mailman, Jake. It was a wet, snowy March morning and we were just moving to the farm from the city. We were standing outside at our neighbors when the mailman pulled up to deliver their mail. "You folks moving in down the road?" he asked. We said we were and introduced ourselves while he assured us we'd like the community and the people around us.

And except for vacations, holidays and no-mail days, we saw Jake nearly every day for 20 years. He delivered the birth announcements of three of our five children; over the years he brought us hundreds of Christmas cards, birthday cards, anniversary cards and sympathy cards.

He delivered everything from trees and garden seeds to baby chickens. Once, I couldn't get to my doctor's office and she mailed a package to me. Jake handed it to me, "Oh, my birth control pills!" I exclaimed unthinking. I thought he was going to choke. Even my weekly newspaper column was picked up by him and sent on its way to the newspaper office to be set in type.

My son, Robbie, carried on a stamp-collection hobby for years through the mail, and Bethany was a pen pal to half a dozen little girls around the world. Our kids received welcome news from Jake as he delivered the letters from the colleges they'd applied to, accepting them into the school and some were accompanied by handsome grants, as well.

Snowy, shut-in days when no-school bulletins were broadcast found me wondering if the mail would run. I'm a lost soul with no daily paper, no grocery ads, no letters, nothing to really sit down, read and enjoy. Many things may come and go - electricity and phone service, but the mail has always gone through. Or at least very nearly always. Jake saw to it.

Jake-the-mailman retired a few years ago. And while we miss seeing his cheery smile, a bright spot in any day is when we hear the sound of the mail carrier's car pulling up to the mailbox. Our world becomes a little larger with the arrival of letters, news magazines, newspapers, letters from our girls away in college, photos of our grandchildren being mailed to us, or examples of their first artworks to post upon the refrigerator.

Saturday Matinee

A recent copy of my hometown newspaper revealed a drive was under way by a local community betterment organization to purchase the old theater that has been closed for years.

The group was seeking pledges of $21,000 to buy the building which was once the Royal Theater; their plans included renovating the building and reopening the theater.

My eyebrows arose as I read the news item while thinking: Now THIS is an idea whose time has finally arrived!

Of all the worthy ventures any civic organization could devise this was one of the best. My hometown, Unionville, Mo., is the county seat of Putnam County, population around 1,900. Like many communities, recent years have seen it take some hard hits economically. But the people down home seem to keep smiling through it all.

In visits to my hometown, my kids often complained that there was nothing to do. And, indeed, there hasn't been. The local roller-skating rink burned down several years ago and was never rebuilt. The Sky-Vue Drive-In Theater is nothing now but a weathered screen, a weed-choked lot and good memories for those of us who went there years ago.

The Royal Theater was closed down so long ago I can't remember when it happened. It was thriving and the focal point of social life when I was in high school and even a few years after I graduated. The last movie I recall seeing at the Royal was a James Bond film. My brother was home on leave from the Marines the fall of 1966, and I was spending a few days with our mother. I was pregnant with my first baby - my memories and family milestones always seem to revolve around whoever I was pregnant with at the time, or which of the kids was a baby.

At the time, in lieu of going out tom-catting around with his high school buddies as he'd planned - the buddies were either married, had moved away, were in college or had other plans - my brother ended up taking his pregnant sister to the Royal.

Some of my fondest memories of growing up revolve around the Royal Theater. There was always the Saturday afternoon matinee to look forward to. A little country girl went to town once a week and besides her grandparents giving her a nickel to spend any way she pleased, she was also given a dime by her mom to go to the show.

And, oh, what movies there were to enjoy. Westerns were probably my favorite, and there was always a serial to look forward to, as well as a news reel which nobody really ever watched, the previews of coming events and the cartoon opener, usually a Looney-Toon.

As I grew older, horror movies were favorites, such as "Godzilla," or "Attack of the Crab People." These usually involved some sort of nuclear incident and the resulting genetic mutations of things like spiders or cockroaches or some other hugely-magnified killer-insect. These movies were creepy and scary and by the age of 12 or 13 the enjoyment of such movies gave way to a whole new element in movie-going: Romance.

A group of 12-and 13-year old girls sitting together watching a horror movie would attract a similar-sized group of boys, and to show his heart's interest, a boy would torment and tease a girl by scaring her, (Boo!) pulling her hair, or subtly throwing a piece of popcorn at her. *Very* subtly - if caught being obnoxious, a kid could get thrown out of the Royal. Even back in the dark ages of the mid-to late-50s, being cool was very important, and being ejected from the theater was definitely not cool.

And what girl can forget the first time she sat with a special boy and felt his arm casually go behind her to rest on the back of the seat only to later drop on her shoulders and stay there?!? And if her girlfriends were witnesses to such daring and True Romance, so much the better!

As I entered high school and later began to date, there was never a question of where to go on Saturday nights, the Royal. And the back row of the theater was the unspoken, yet well known, designated seating area for Serious Couples to discreetly snuggle and watch Doris Day and Rock Hudson; Martin and Lewis; Sandra Dee and John Gavin; Jeff Chandler, Cary Grant, and be still my beating heart, Elvis!

Every dating couple had a special place where they sat every Saturday night and everyone knew it. Only strangers would sit in those spots. Or grown-ups who didn't know any better, but were politely tolerated by the rest of us despite their ignorance.

Myron and Marjorie Woolever ran the theater. They were always friendly and courteous and very patient with kids. But woe unto anyone who misbehaved. I *know* I never got in trouble, and I'm *pretty* sure my brother never did - or at least never got caught. Myron and Marjorie were friends of Mama's and she would have found out if we hadn't behaved. In fact, the Woolevers were friends with nearly everyone, so sooner or later a person's misdeeds would catch up with them.

Those were, I suppose, the early lessons of correct social behavior, conscience and yes, possibly even moral conduct - all learned at the Royal.

I've noticed a decline in those values with the closing of small town theaters. Many kids today have never had a Royal Theater in their life, with its undefined yet very important code of behavior. Most kids don't have a Myron or a Margorie to watch over their behavior, notice new hairdos, wink if they notice a new boyfriend, or congratulate a kid on winning a blue ribbon at the county fair.

Yes, I think my hometown is on the right track with this theater project.

Few kids with Saturday matinee memories can be anything other that public-spirited citizens and good Americans. I predict great things for my hometown if the Royal is reborn.

photo by Bob Nandell

Blue-jeans housewife

Housewifery

Along with the California condor and the Tennessee snail darter, I sometimes feel I'm part of a vanishing species.

I'm what is generally known as "just a housewife"

There are many reasons why I haven't joined the work force. The biggest one is my husband, Bob. He happens to be one of those fossils, an unliberated, male, chauvinist porker, and is very unashamed of his condition.

He is not a particular admirer of Phil Donahue, Alan Alda or Jane Fonda. If found reading a glossy-paged men's magazine of questionable taste and literary value, he will be the first to admit that the articles are the last-read features. He views the gay rights movement with disgust and alarm. He believes in capital punishment for murderers and child molesters and corporal punishment for his offspring.

And not to put too fine a line on it, he wants his wife, me, at home browning hamburger, patching jeans, sewing a fine seam, baking cookies, cleaning house and involved in good works.

My children, too, agree with their dad that they like Mom at home. They enjoy the fruits of my labor - the snacks, cookies and sometimes even the smell of freshly-baked bread and cinnamon rolls when they come home from school. If they get sick at school or forget to bring the science project - a jar full of crawly ants or half-dead jellified tadpoles - rescue is no further than a phone call home.

The times they've come home to an empty, unmommed house, I've been greeted later with accusatory alarm, "Where were you?! Why weren't you home? We were worried!" My little girls, particularly, are upset if I'm not home when they arrive from school with stories to tell me about their day at school. The boys are partially mollified at what they deem unnatural, unmaternal behavior on my part if there's food around.

And last, but certainly not the least of the reasons I have chosen the role of housewife is ME. I enjoy the job. I like working at my own pace with the sound of the radio in the background. I like finding something new to do with hamburger. It's a treat to be able to do something that pleases and surprises my family - that is, if I feel they're deserving and I'm in the right mood - as I did on a recent day by making doughnuts from scratch, something I'd never tried before.

I enjoy doing laundry on a sunny, breezy day and hanging sheets and towels on the clothesline, or washing windows, or deciding out of the blue that, yes indeed, I will paint the walls of the bedroom, or clean the basement or defrost the deep freeze.

If I want to I can and do plant a half-acre garden and a large strawberry bed, and be assured that I'll have the time and energy to care for it. I'll can and freeze the extra and have some to share, too, with friends who aren't as fortunate as I.

Since I'm a comparatively disorganized, uncoordinated person, I don't see how I could hold down a job and be a housewife, too. I could never be one of those super women of whom I've read. Why, I'm so scatter-brained that if I talk on the phone while I'm scrubbing a pan, I'll likely find the Chore Girl scrubber in the refrigerator the next time I clean it. (It's happened before.) Or the paring knife I'm using to peel potatoes as I talk with one of the kids will wind up in the flour canister.

I'm not particularly skilled for any career. I haven't the patience to be a teacher's aide, nor the stomach to be a nurse's aide. As a retail clerk I couldn't tolerate the rude treatment by customers. School bus driving is out - I'd smack the first mouthy, dirty-talking kid that crossed me, and besides, I'm scared of winter driving. I can't run for an elected office, afraid that I wouldn't win the election, but more afraid that I would.

So I'm left with what I consider the important and gratifying position of full-time housewife and sometime scribe.

Oh, I'll admit there are times I envy my friends their jobs away from home with their nice clothes, styled hair and makeup skillfully applied to seemingly tireless faces. Their two-paycheck homes are furnished beautifully while I look at my own stuff, mismatched with sagging springs and lampshades with crayon marks. And their vacations are taken to wonderful-sounding places. My kids try not to envy their kids for the mopeds, video games, multiple pairs of Nike shoes and no hand-me-down clothes.

On gray, drizzly, gloomy days, especially, I sometimes wish I worked away from home - those days when my brain feels dull and underused, like a slice of moldy bread; when I'm bored and hungry to talk to someone over 15 and on some subject besides the price of a lunch ticket or cures for athlete's foot. When I feel like that, however, I know that someday the sun will shine again and then I'll be glad I'm home doing what I do best.

I hear my more liberated friends groaning, "Oh no, your thinking is completely out of line, Linda. I suppose you even polish your husband's shoes?"

Well, as a matter of fact, yes.

But only if he says, "please."

Medora Ladies Aid *photo by Bob Nandell*

Quilting Generations

We went to a church fund-raiser pancake breakfast the other day. The men of the church were flipping pancakes, frying sausage and lacy-edged, over-easy eggs. Personally, I can think of few sights as satisfying as seeing a man with an apron wrapped around his middle and a spatula in his hand.

And as the men served breakfast, the good ladies of the church watched from the sidelines seated around a quilt-in-progress, a craft for which the ladies at the church are noted.

Upon seeing this, Jenny squealed, “Oh how cool! A quilt. I didn’t think people did that anymore, Mom!” And she and her sister went over to get a closer look at the quilt.

She was nearly right. Not many people do quilt anymore, or at least not in the traditional way, which is piecing a quilt together and assembling it into a quilt frame as it awaits to be hand-stitched, many times using intricate patterns with leaves and vines intertwined.

I came from a family of quilters. At least once a year my mom had a quilt set up in our living room when I was a kid. If it wasn’t an annual occurrence, at least it *seemed* like it.

The setting up of her quilt always coincided with the meeting of her club, the Stringtown Extension Club, being held at our house.

Mama would work for weeks, indeed months, piecing together a quilt using scraps of material from her sewing projects. In fact, our family history can practically be traced through the fabrics she used in her quilt patterns. "Now this was from the pajamas I made your brother when he had appendicitis," she'll remark, or "This is from the dress you made in 4-H that time it went to the state fair and got a blue ribbon...and this material was from that apron Grandma liked so much...and this is from those matching dresses I made for us, remember?"

And on club day as the ladies met in our home for their meeting and potluck lunch, they would sit around the quilt stitching and chatting. In a blur of motion a quilter could bite off a piece of thread and rethread a needle without blinking an eye.

The one cloud on my horizon during this whole process was that the ladies would never completely finish quilting a quilt on club day. The quilt would remain it its wooden frame while I bumped against it and tripped over the kitchen chairs sitting around it for weeks to come. And try throwing school books or laying anything else on the quilt. Well! Wouldn't we have a tizzy! "You're going to get it dirty and cause the quilt to sag!" my mom would scold.

Life as we knew it ceased while the quilt and its frame were sitting in the living room. It took up most of the space and a kid had to slide in sideways just to get to the kitchen. To watch TV was nearly impossible since you either had to duck your head to look under the quilt or stand up to look over it.

It was always a good sign when a little bit more quilting had been accomplished allowing the quilt to be rolled up in its frame a little more creating more space in the room. My brother and I actively encouraged Mama to invite neighbor ladies in to spend an afternoon quilting which might speed things on.

My mom didn't allow me to work on her quilt when I was little. That's what grandmas are for. Grandmas will let a little girl do stuff that moms won't. And when my grandma had her quilt set up in her dining room she allowed me to help her quilt, patiently teaching me how to make tiny stitches. "You want to make tiny little stitches on a quilt," she said, "And that way they're not big enough to get your toenails caught in." And that made quite a lot of sense. I was probably 40 before I thought about it and realized that no decent homemaker in our family would have allowed a quilt on a bed without at least a bedsheet beneath it and a bedspread on top to protect it. So how would stitches of any size snag a toenail? But that's another thing grandmas do is tell funny stories.

A fond memory I have is sitting beside my grandma in her dining room on a snowy winter afternoon. Grandpa was in the living room gently snoring as he slept in his chair with the newspaper laying on his lap. Grandma's old clock was making its tick-tock sounds in the background as she and I stitched and chattered.

A week or so ago we went to my mom's for a visit. She had something to show me, she said, and led me to a back bedroom. And there, leaning against the wall was a rolled-up quilt she had been working on. She'd taken it down from its place in the living room and rolled it up, she said, because she was having company.

My daughters expressed interest in the quilt since they had seen the one at the church the morning of the pancake breakfast. While I was peevishly wondering why quilts couldn't have been rolled up and put out of the way when I was a kid, I heard my mom offering to teach the girls about quilting.

Funny, I've offered to teach them about some of the arts of needlework such as embroidery and quilting and they turned up their noses. Suddenly, they want to learn.

But from their grandma.

It must be one of those generation things.

Legacy Of A One-Room School House

School Days - 1953. Cousins Sandy and Sue, me and my brother, Mike.

A recent cartoon strip of "The Family Circus" showed Dad and the kids out for a walk in the woods when they stumbled across a dilapidated old schoolhouse.

"An old abandoned one-room schoolhouse," Dad said, while Jeffy observed, "Wonder what ever became of the poor little kids who had to go to school there?" And hovering over the school were the grown-up "ghosts" of the students or "poor little kids" who had attended the school: a sailor, a fireman, nurse, judge, a CEO, a ball player, astronaut, orchestra conductor, artist, an Army general, a preacher and a chemist to name a few; so many people who had received their early lessons in a humble one-room schoolhouse.

And although it wasn't noted in the cartoon, a writer could also have been depicted coming from a one-room schoolhouse.

You're reading the words of a person who received most of her education in a one-room schoolhouse in Missouri, taught for the most part by a state-certified teacher and not necessarily one with a college degree.

We were taught a broad range of subjects: American history, world history, Missouri history, civics, science, horticulture, agriculture, math, reading, grammar, geography, art and health and hygiene.

We had to memorize the preambles to the Missouri and U.S. constitutions, the Bill of Rights of each, the Declaration of Independence, the

Gettysburg Address, as well as an endless list of poems, math formulas and tables, quotes and entire plays.

Besides that, we were taught to respect our teacher, show courtesy to one another (when possible), cooperation, sharing and how to play a decent game of softball without short stops or an outfield, using only one cracked and taped bat, a ratty softball and a baseball glove only if someone brought theirs from home. We shared the water dipper, sack lunches, games, secrets and books. Lunch times were wonderful times to learn about commerce and trade. A fried egg sandwich could be traded for cake, and an apple or grapes for an orange.

It was considered an honor to be appointed by the teacher to carry in drinking water from the well or to help spread sweeping compound before cleaning the floors. Big boys were asked to help bring in coal for the stove and girls were in charge of keeping little first-graders entertained when the weather kept everyone inside during recess.

There were four students in my eighth grade class and we had only two history books. Jerry and Hubert sat together to study their book; my cousin Sue and I sat and shared the other book, only occasionally getting into fits of giggles when we would be separated by the teacher and marched up to sit with the first grade. It didn't do a thing for our self esteem, but did teach us a lesson on classroom behavior.

There were no such things as peer helpers or cadet teachers, but the older students took turns from their studies or free time to help younger students with reading or spelling, freeing the teacher to do something else.

Our recesses and lunch hours were times for all-school athletic contests, and in bad weather or special times like Friday afternoons, we had highly competitive and entertaining spelling, math and geography contests to look forward to. I can remember scribbling math solutions with squeaking chalk on a blackboard. The faces of Abraham Lincoln and George Washington looked sternly down at me from their pictures atop the chalkboard.

Schoolyard ghosts.

I well remember the days once or twice a month when the bookmobile from the public library visited bringing in fresh books to be enjoyed. And to also be reported on in English class using good handwriting, correct grammar and spelling. None of this "graded on content only" stuff as is done in many schools today, but the book report was graded on everything from penmanship to spelling to grammar, as well as neatness. (And my kids wonder where I come by all my ideas on what constitutes a book report or an essay?)

Oh, and students had no rights then. The teacher was the boss and there was no back talk or other disrespectful behavior. If there was punishment, it was meted out swiftly from the teacher and then at home when parents learned of their student's misdeed. There was no disciplinary hearing except for the one in front of the teacher's desk.

And those "good old days" didn't occur in the 1930s or 1940s as some might suspect. I was fortunate to go to a one-room grade school before they were closed. Our school closed down and the students were bused to school in town after I entered high school - it was 1960 or 1961, I believe. Iowa had closed its one-room schools much earlier than Missouri.

With memories of what I learned in my school, I don't believe even with all the technology, computers, calculators, special education programs and teachers' paperwork that kids today get a better education than I received. In fact, sometimes quite the opposite is true.

I don't know if it's the teachers, the curriculum, over-educated, insecure eggheads who come up with new teaching "tools" or concepts every year, or government intrusion which has caused the regression of education. I know only that I feel fortunate to have experienced the lessons taught in a little brown stucco schoolhouse with a school yard landscaped in mowed alfalfa and orchard grass, graced by a pitcher's mound and squeaking playground swings.

I was lucky to be a "poor little kid."

Those were good times.

Neighbor girl and her lamb. *photo by Bob Nandell*

Shepherd

I very seldom do any great in-depth reading of the ag sections of newspapers. In the first place, we don't farm. Oh sure, we live in the country, but we grow no row crops or livestock.

And farming today doesn't seem to be even remotely related to the farming done when I was a kid. Back then, farm families pretty much lived on what they earned and grew on the farm. And their kids worked on the farm, too, beside their moms and dads.

All in all, it was a pretty good life.

But an article in the paper about the production of sheep caught my eye recently. I read it and remembered my own tender years on the farm when we raised sheep.

I don't remember when my mom became interested in getting our family in the sheep-raising business. It probably had something to do with her farm-advisor, my uncle Kenneth, who lived next to us. He was a smooth-talking yet lovable hustler who was always getting into deals of one nature or another. If I recall correctly he got in the sheep business about the same time we did, and chances are the two were connected. All I know is that one day my brother and I came home from school and there they were: sheep; twenty-five ewes of varying breeds and lambing season was about to commence.

Over the years most of the ewes became pets, nearly members of the family, and every one of them had a personality. There was Stoopie, short for Stupid. She didn't have brains enough to care for any baby she ever had and abandoned them. But she was crafty enough to butt open a locked gate letting into the garden and yard every bit of livestock we had, milk cows, the other sheep, and even chickens. And they caused messes and damage that could get a young girl chewed out by her mom for leaving the gate open. But Stoopie had known just the right spot on the gate to butt with just the right amount of pressure to pop the gate fastener loose. Into the yard the ewe would triumphantly and smugly march.

Pixie was another unique ewe. She was neat and dainty, possessing a masked black face and black legs. If a sheep could be called pretty, she was. But she was a snob and wouldn't mix with any of the rest of the herd. When she had a lamb, she and her baby would keep themselves apart from the rest of the sheep. While the other lambs were frolicking and hopping around as young playful lambs do, Pixie's lamb would stay by her side and haughtily watch the juvenile carryings-on of other lambs.

Lambing season was always a special time of the year for a kid. And I could think that since it was mostly my mom who got up in the middle of the night to check on the sheep to see if any had had their lambs, or were trying to, but were having trouble and needed help. I can remember a few times, though, getting rousted out of bed on a cold night (lambing season never seems to occur in mild weather) to go to the shed where the sheep were locked up for the night and check on them, or help bring a stubborn baby into the world.

There's a special nice, warm sheep smell that I still remember - a smell of hay and wool and warmth - and that deep-down-in-the-throat bleat of a ewe nuzzling a fresh-born lamb.

Occasionally there would be twin lambs and that was always a treat. More often than I like to think there were triplet lambs, and that meant bottle-feeding one or all of them to supplement the ewe's milk. That's when we'd get one of Uncle Kenneth's whiskey bottles (he had a fondness for an occasional nip or 10) and use them for baby bottles.

Or an unnatural ewe - like Stoopie - would not claim her baby and we'd be left with a dead lamb or one that was kept in a box in the kitchen to bottle feed, or as sometimes happened, watch it weaken and die. That was always hard. Hard for us kids because we loved lambs, and hard on our mom because that meant a lamb which couldn't be sold.

Pet lambs were just a fact of life in our family - there were always two or three that were bottle-fed and became pets who wanted their ears scratched as they butted the bottle in enthusiasm, knocked their heads playfully into our knees, or stood baaing at the kitchen door wanting to be let in as if they were house cats. And if one did by chance make its way into the kitchen with its hard little pointy hooves, it would sound as if little old lady in high heels were click-clicking across the kitchen linoleum.

I can think of no other animal quite so comical and playful as a lamb. It was always a sad day when my brother and I came home from school and found the lambs had been sold.

We raised and sold sheep, but to this day I have never tasted mutton or lamb. It's been more than 30 years since I've held a woolly lamb in my arms or wrestled a stubborn old ewe through a barn lot gate. But if I had to eat mutton or lamb, I'd feel like I'd just consumed the family pooch.

photo by Bob Nandell

The In-Service Heirloom

I was scrubbing the kitchen sink for probably the millionth time when Bob noticed what I was doing. He walked over and chuckling, said, "Of all the things we could give the kids from this house, the kitchen sink would tell the most stories."

"What do you mean?" I asked.

"Well, look at it. That sink's been used so much, and you've scrubbed it so many times, the porcelain is wearing off. You don't see that happen with a sink very often," he explained.

And yes, I suppose he was right. If our sink could talk, it could tell many stories.

It seems that life in our house sometimes seems to revolve around the kitchen and the kitchen sink.

The sink was installed in 1973 some months after we'd moved into our new home after living *beneath* it in the basement for two years as we painstakingly tried to complete the upstairs. We finally determined to move upstairs despite the fact there were no kitchen cabinets, nor sink. There was a stove, a refrigerator and a table. The rest would get finished later. "Later" never did arrive completely. The cabinets Bob built "until we can get better ones," are still there, and the sink we purchased is the same one that has been in our kitchen for 23 years.

And while we replaced both the stove and refrigerator with new ones in recent years, the sink has remained. The faucet has been changed a couple of times when leaks or cracks have developed, but the sink, chipped and with its white finish dimming, has remained.

It has seen near-constant use. I wonder how many thousands of dishes have been washed in it? We had a dishwasher for years - still do, only it doesn't work - but washing the dishes in the sink always seemed to get the job done better. My mom has always maintained that the best visiting can be done over a sink of dirty dishes as they are washed and wiped dry. For years, she and I had a third member working with us, usually directing our efforts, when my grandmother was still well and accompanied Mama to visit us. Or perhaps after dinner would be the time Grandma would take a little nap, and Mama and I would do the dishes, quietly talking between us so Grandma was not disturbed from her rest.

"What was that you just said?" we'd hear coming from where she was laying down, and we'd know that she was always with us one way or the other - either with a tea towel or keen hearing.

That scuffed-up old sink was used for bathing new babies and also was just the right size for chubby toddlers; I have photos of each of my girls sitting in a suds-filled kitchen sink, big smiles on their faces, new teeth peeking out, and I remember those times when the sink served as a bathtub.

I remember when the girls were little and wanted to help with dishes. I would pull up a chair for them to stand on and tie a dish towel around each of them as an apron and splatter-catcher. They got to "help" with the plastic bowls and spoons and felt so grown up as they splashed happily in the dish water.

That eagerness to help with the dishes seemed to change by the time they were in high school, however.

When the boys were teen-agers, the sink was likely to be filled with the corpses of dead animals, evidence of the marksmanship of my young hunters and their dad. "You killed it, you clean it," was the rule, which didn't always work. And a number of times I was left with a gory disgusting mess to deal with, like the stringers of fish I'd find that still needed to be cleaned. That doesn't count the dozens of chickens I raised and butchered in one of my many back-to-the-earth modes the family endured.

I remember my brother once bringing a girlfriend down from the city to the farm, and I had chickens which had been plucked, cleaned and cut into pieces soaking in water on one side of the sink. On the other side, I had a pan of chicken innards and generally unpleasant-looking poultry parts ready to throw out. I still recall the young woman's reaction of horror when she went to the sink for a drink of water.

I wonder if she ever got over her aversion to chicken after that?

The springtime will find the sink filled with mushrooms soaking in salt water if we've had any luck finding them, that is. Later on, strawberries will be washed and stemmed at the sink; green beans and sweet corn will fill it in the summer and in the fall, tomatoes, green peppers and onions will rest in it as I make salsa and relishes.

Heated words have been exchanged between Bob and me when I've had occasion to find gooey, oily, automotive things he's left soaking in the sink, leaving behind a grimy residue stinking of gasoline. When my back is turned, dogs and even cats have been shampooed in the sink with burs and matted hair balls left behind on the back of the sink while the smell of wet fur lingers, I'd swear, for days afterward.

In that banged-up old sink I have washed the kids' bloody wounds from various mishaps, as well as hoisted them up to wash off small, muddy, bare feet tracking in from outdoors.

I have cried, I suppose, not a few tears over the sink, and have nestled the phone in the crook of my neck while listening to a caller even as I've washed dishes or scoured the sink. While I'll admit to being a somewhat slap-dash housekeeper, I do like a shiny, clean, white sink, cleared of stains and scum, even if I'm revealing its diminishing porcelain.

I've nagged Bob for years about wanting to get the kitchen redone. And I suppose when the time comes, the old sink will be replaced, but a little of the soul of the place will be missing when the old one is removed.

(The old sink was removed and thrown out in the spring of '97 when I got my long-promised new kitchen.)

My Grandpa, Carl Pollock, at chore time.

Something In The Air

I think the nose and the brain are more closely connected than any other organs. A certain scent can send one's mind to another place, another time. Emotions can be stirred, thoughts and memories created or replayed. And all because something is in the air.

Bob and I were enjoying a walk early one summer evening in our ritual stroll down to our pond several hundred feet from the house. A path is mowed through the hay field for our walks and an area around the pond is also kept mowed. An old wooden park bench in need of a fresh coat of paint sits on the pond bank. Nearby is a cottonwood tree which keeps us company by the constant rustling of its leaves even on days when there seems to be no air stirring. The pond is the place where members of our family go to meditate when the soul needs some time to itself, or the mind needs some quiet from a sometimes frantic and noisy day.

The sun hadn't yet set, but it was that still and quiet part of the day when even nature seems to wind down a bit. There was a bit of a breeze and the barn swallows were out swooping down to the pond's surface, scooping up water or catching waterbugs - I'm never sure which.

The lightning bugs were beginning to flicker and a few stars were popping out in the evening sky. Frogs were jumping into the pond ahead of our uninvited companion, our cocker spaniel Mitzi, who loves the water and tries to catch frogs while her furry, mop-like paws plopped along the muddy water's edge making her sound like a Clydesdale.

As Bob and I stood on a rise of ground above the pond surveying our kingdom with contentment, I took a deep breath, smelling the air around me.

It was a sweet, summertime smell, a smell of growing things and flowers. The scent of red clover, Queen Anne's lace and even ragweed was filling the air.

It's a green and earthy and woodsy smell, something the most creative perfumery could not duplicate. To me it's also a memory-smell. It took my mind back through the years as I explained to Bob where my memory-journey was taking me:

To my grandparents' place in north central Missouri, a place I still remember as if I had visited it yesterday.

My grandparents' farm was across the county from ours. I would stay with them any time I had a chance. And when I stayed with them in the summertime, my grandpa let me help with the chores. Oh, I had chores at home, but helping Grandma and Grandpa with chores was always more fun. They made it more interesting and made me feel like I was the smartest and most helpful person around. And while we did chores, they would talk to me and tell me stories about whatever it was that we were doing.

One of my favorite things to do was go out in the pasture with Grandpa and bring in the cows for milking. Most evenings they automatically came up to the barn by themselves, instinctively knowing it was milking-time. But anyone who has ever had anything to do with cows knows how independent they can be. Or they get interested in something else, like standing under a mulberry tree chewing their cuds, or finding a new patch of grass to graze on, or sometimes staying away just out of contrariness.

Those were the times when we had to go out into the pasture and drive them home to the barn and the waiting empty milk buckets.

I can still see my grandpa in his sweat-stained straw hat, wearing bib overalls, a patched and faded blue chambray shirt and scuffed, brown lace-up work shoes, as he took his walking stick, and we would head out to get the cows. I would trot beside him, bare-footed, summer-tanned and brown-legged and jabber at him, asking him questions about everything. "You're a regular Windy Wallops," he would call me and chuck me under the chin and tell me to keep on with my chatter.

He would answer all my questions or make up funny stories about things as he told me about fence building, or Tom his old work horse, or the finer points of his beloved Angus beef cattle, or tales when he was a young boy in the horse and buggy days at the turn of the century. He was fun to tease, too, and I picked him bouquets of flowers, including his much-hated chicory, the blue-flowered weed growing on roadsides, which also choked his barn lot causing him quite a lot of frustration -he could never get rid of it. He hated chicory, so I teased him about it and called it Grandpa's bachelor button, a domestic flower it resembles. (He was probably around 90 and the farm had been sold many years the last time I picked him a bouquet like that and joked with him once again as he chuckled warmly at our shared memory of wildflowers and weeds lovingly dressed up as a little girl's love-gift for her grandpa.)

But as my grandpa and I got the cows and headed for home, the smell in the fields was one of clover and Queen Anne's lace and ragweed. It was a good smell that I never particularly noticed at the time, but have recalled again and again over the years.

The cows would take their time walking down winding cow paths that had been there since God created Missouri, I swear. With their tails swishing, hocks cracking and an occasional saucy toss of the head to let us know they were returning to the barn because it was what they wanted to do, not because we were driving them, we slowly made it back to the barn. "Don't want to hurry them," my grandpa explained. "They won't give any milk." So we made allowances for temperamental behavior.

And as I shared my memories with Bob during our evening walk and again sniffed the air, it struck me that scented memories are the very best kind, whether its the smell of a hayfield taking me back to when I was about 10 years old walking beside my grandpa, the scent of lilacs bringing memories of my high school sweetheart, or the smell of baby powder prompting memories of giving baths to my babies.

Nose memories are the best memories.

Sadie, the latest family mutt. *photo by Bob Nandell*

Old Snooks

For the first time in many, many years our family does not have a dog.

My little Toby-dog was hit and killed by a car last winter; and Prince, our faithful yet lazy collie was a victim of last summer's heat.

I had allowed myself to become fond of those two dogs - something I try not to do. But it seems I have a weak spot for some dogs, particularly those with a certain twinkle in the eye. This was first apparent with a dog we had when I was a kid, Old Snooks.

Snooks was the runt of a 1954 litter of pups. He was a cute, sweet-natured, not-terribly-smart mixed breed - very mixed, with some wire-haired terrier, maybe some cocker. He could've been a little of anything. Except poodle. There were no poodles in the hill country of Missouri where I grew up. I doubt if there are any to this day.

The only kind of dog a decent God-fearing person would have would be a collie or a hunting dog like a coon hound. But our family had Snooks, and oh how we loved that little white-haired dog with the brown spot of his back.

Old Snooks accompanied my brother Mike and me on many of our adventures. He followed us on all of our travels over the hills and creeks of the countryside and when we got home he'd flop down and snooze.

He was a valued member of our family. So valued that when he was caught sucking eggs, instead of getting shot, he was given a pepper egg. It was fun to watch our mom fix up a hollow eggshell with Tabasco and cay-enne - anything hot and burny-tasting went into the eggshell, and it was set out for Snooks to find.

We watched as Snooks stealthily grabbed the forbidden morsel and took off with it. "We'll teach him to suck eggs," we thought. But you know after watching him bite into the hot-pepper egg and go off yelping and rubbing his nose and tongue on the ground, it didn't seem nearly so funny. But better a burnt mouth than a dead dog, we figured. And he never messed with the hen house or eggs again.

There was a time when Mama went out to the coal shed early one morning to get a bucket of coal. She came scurrying back to the house with no coal. There was a mean old hissing she-coon in the coal shed, she said.

My brother and I ran out, peeked in the door and hurriedly ducked back out. "Yep, she's right. There's a coon in there, a mean one, too! Let's run across the field and get Grandpa, he'll take care of it."

So across the field we went to get our no-nonsense great-grandpa. We excitedly told him what had happened as he slowly pushed back from the breakfast table. Reaching for his squirrel gun and his cane, he called his dogs, Puff, a terrier, and Pup, a half-grown, clumsy collie-mutt.

Off we went, Grandpa, my brother and me, surrounded by dogs, back to our place to deal with the problem of the coon in the coal shed. Grandpa wasn't worried about the coon and had brought his rifle merely for reserve. The front-line troops were to be craven Puff, stupid Pup and our beloved Snooks. Grandpa pitched the dogs in the coal shed and shut the door.

Silence.

And then there came the most gawdawful racket with yelps, screeches, whines and hissing. The coal shed siding was shaking, a couple of boards came loose, and coal dust filtered through the cracks. After about five minutes the noise died down and all was quiet.

Grandpa grabbed his cane and his gun, went over and opened the door. Three dogs came tearing out and weren't seen again for the rest of the day. We later found the coon, covered with coal dust; quite dead, of course.

And so our love for Snooks grew over the years as he followed us around at chore time; as he followed Mike rabbit hunting, watched him build model airplanes, learn to drive a car and finally came the day Snooks stood at the end of the driveway wagging his tail and watching as Mike went off and joined the Marines later winding up in a nasty little piece of real estate in Southeast Asia.

Old Snooks watched as I played house, had bike wrecks, and wore my first high heels. He embarrassed me half to death by barking menacingly at my first date. He walked me to the school bus, slept on a freshly-pressed graduation gown and I tripped over him on my way out the door on my wedding day.

The years passed and one small white-haired dog witnessed the changes.

Then Snooks was missing one weekend when we were home for a visit. We figured he'd been caught in a fence somewhere and we missed him and his greeting.

It was the spring of 1967 and the snow was melting. I'd had my first baby in February. Bob and I were at the farm where I was raised when we decided to leave the baby with his grandma and go for a walk down the country road I'd traipsed along growing up.

We were returning from our walk when I happened to look in the ditch and saw something. At first it looked like a pile of unmelted snow. And then I saw the brown spot.

It had been several years since I'd thought of Snooks as the dear friend and companion he'd always been; until I saw him laying there in that ditch.

That is why I try not to become overly fond of dogs. I used up all my love for dogs when I was a young girl.

And all for a scruffy-looking little white dog with a twinkle in his eyes.

Donald, the sorghum-maker.

The Fine Art Of Sorghum-Making

An autumn visit with relatives in my home state of Missouri found me once again embarking on a new adventure. This time I helped my cousin make sorghum, that thick, brown, sticky sweetener that tastes so special on fresh-from-the-oven cornbread or even when licked off the end of a piece of sugar cane that's been dipped into a large vat of the bubbling, nearly-ready stuff.

My cousin, Donald, who probably should've been born a century ago, built himself a sorghum mill. Given the propensity and breeds of various state and federal revenuers, safety, health and food inspection people, I'm not real sure I could even recall where exactly in Missouri my cousin built his mill. I get all mixed up in directions and can never tell if a place is toward Kansas City or St. Louis; whether it looks toward Iowa or is next to Arkansas.

The mill probably wouldn't pass government standards, in fact, I'm sure it wouldn't. It is, after all, an honest-to-God, old-fashioned mill with no screen wire near it, no hairnets in evidence, (or even beard-nets), and there's no fire extinguishers either, or other safety equipment so the Feds from OSHA would certainly have a good time. But the fact of the matter is, my cousin makes darned good sorghum using centuries-old techniques, and I had a chance to watch it being made and even helped pour it off.

For those who would like to know about it, and I'm sure there are scores who would, I'll describe as best I can the art of Missouri sorghum-making.

Sorghum cane is grown in the poor soil of the hill country. Rich soil will not grow good cane, I'm told. Oh, the cane will be fine; but the cane juice will not make good sorghum which my cousin learned to his grief a year or two ago.

The cane is cut and brought in by the wagon load and put through a press that squeezes the juice into a large galvanized garbage can. Then, using a Sears and Roebuck sump pump and a garden hose, the can full of juice is pumped up a slight hill to fill a large galvanized stock tank. Here comes a really strange part when two five-gallon buckets of Missouri hill-side clay are dumped into the squeezin's. All the fiber, assorted crud and impurities that have stayed with the cane juice cling to the clay and the whole mess sinks to the bottom of the tank, leaving the rest to be siphoned off (using PVC pipe the local rural water project forgot to pick up) and run down hill to the large vat that's setting on top of a brick-walled, coffin-shaped fire hole. The fire hole has sand filling one end that, when hot, stays hot, enabling the syrup to cook evenly. A hot wood fire fills the other end of the 4- by 12-foot fire hole. The entire set-up is housed under a tin-roofed structure with no walls.

There's a smell in the air of hickory smoke and cooking cane juice that is unmatched anywhere as far as I'm concerned.

The watery juice is cooked down until only about 10 percent of it is remaining in the form of sorghum. The process takes about 12 hours and usually yields from 15 to 20 gallons of the finished product which can be sold for around $16 a gallon. Only my cousin doesn't sell sorghum, you understand. He sells the container and if the container happens to have sorghum in it, that's the problem of the buyer. Not having a retail license or any such thing he couldn't legally sell the stuff, now could he?

There's excitement as the time comes when the sorghum is nearing completion as it boils up on a beautiful, taffy-colored foam. When the bubbles are the size of sheep's eyes, (My mom said she dreamed of sheep eyeballs the night after we helped make sorghum.) the sorghum is ready to be poured into containers, first being strained of any foreign material that hasn't gone up in steam

Neighbors sniffing the sorghum smell in the air drive up or walk in and watch the process as my cousin, his wife, daughter, son-in-law and any assorted cousin who happens to be around slide the vat off the fire hole, tip and pour it into containers that are taken to a safe, clean place to cool off and are later poured into individual smaller containers.

My cousin grows his own cane. Occasionally people hear of his mill and ask him about processing their cane. One cantankerous old guy from a neighboring county, we were told, had grown cane for the first time this year. But he hadn't grown it for its potential sorghum content. No, he'd grown it for his neighbor's livestock. It seems his neighbor's cattle were always getting into his field. This year, he thought, he'd teach the neighbor a lesson about fence-mending by planting cane in the field that the neighbor's stock liked. They'd once again get out, eat their fill and die. No more problem. Only this year the livestock didn't get out and he was left with a field of cane.

My mom, the little girls and I laughed over that story on the way home that night. We were full of cane juice, sorghum and laughter. We smelled like wood smoke and syrup; felt dusty, sticky and smeary, and our tongues were sore from the sugary, boiling hot syrup we'd tasted.

But we'd had a good time, instilling in my daughters a deeper sense of family and more memories to store up to tell their children of the night of the sorghum makin'.

Hometown News

I ran into a lady in the grocery store recently - I had first met her years ago when I spoke at her club meeting. With her was another woman, who although I could not recall meeting before, seemed as though she knew me. In fact, she and I had never met. She lives in Washington state and her mother, who was with her at the grocery store, subscribes to the RHT for her, as well as her brother who also lives far away. These Warren County natives keep up with the news back home through their hometown newspaper. While doing so they read this column which has acquainted not a few people with me and my family, as well as some of our views on things going on around us. No wonder she acted like she knew me. She practically does.

My mom subscribes to my hometown paper for me and my brother, too. It's in such a way through that community newspaper, the Unionville Republican, that I find out a bit of what is going on in one of the most important places in the world to me. And that is the place where I was born and raised.

Through reading the obituaries, I can find out who has died, who conducted the funeral service and who were the pall-bearers. I also find out who have become parents - more often than not these days I look to see who the grandparents or great-grandparents are. The cards of thanks are revealing and tell me who has been sick, who has had their soybeans harvested by neighbors or who has had some other kindness performed for them by friends and neighbors. In the court news, I can find out who has been caught with drugs, who is getting divorced and what the settlement terms are and who has bounced a check.

A history feature, "Down Memory Lane," tells me what was on the pages of the Republican 10 or 20 or 30 or 40 years ago. It's the 30 and 40 years ago part that usually catches my eye. And there are the "locals," news items of who is visiting whom, who had a birthday party, returned from vacation or attended an out of town funeral.

Readers recently found out that I visited my mother on a Friday and helped her do fall chores. It didn't add that we pickled 18 pints of beets, I dug her canna bulbs and tore out a bunch of viney stuff, and got to eat Mama's great pot roast. We also visited my grandmother at the nursing home and I made her laugh.

The paper had a brief mention of a couple of changes in the business district, the town square, which caused me to spend quite a few moments reminiscing. A news item said that the marquee was being covered at the city library, which had recently moved into the former movie theater.

That marquee had once announced the dates and times and titles of movies - it had been the marquee of The Royal Theater. The Royal was once THE place for a Saturday afternoon matinee if you were a kid, and the place everyone under the age of 25 went on Saturday and Sunday nights.

It was there I saw matinees with my friends as we watched monster movies and westerns starring Audie Murphy and Randolph Scott when a ticket cost a dime. Abbott and Costello and the Bowery Boys entertained us, as well as cartoons of "Tweety and Sylvester" and "Tom and Jerry."

Later during high school, the Royal was where a dating pair was first noticed as a couple. The Royal was the place we went to see so-called adult movies - tame offerings now compared with what my kids can see on TV any weekday or night. We saw "Peyton Place," and "A Summer Place," and was there ever such a handsome couple as Troy Donahue and Sandra Dee? And what did she ever see in Bobby Darrin anyway?

The Royal had a summertime counterpart - the Sky-Vue Drive-In which has been closed many, many years.

The Royal has been closed for years, too. One of its last movies was "Jaws" back in the mid-70s, but its marquee always remained and later heralded sales when it housed a retail clothing store. And now the marquee will disappear and nobody will suspect that the brick building on the east side of the town square was once the site of so much activity and social speculation.

The second business item was the announcement that a "Closed" sign was now on the door of the Ben Franklin store. As far as I'm concerned, that spells the end of what was once a booming business district in my hometown.

Why, the Ben Franklin store is where a kid once could expect to find her mom after the matinee was over at The Royal. It was the place you could find anything in the world to buy from wallpaper to clothing to dinner dishes. That's where kids bought presents for their moms for Christmas and Mother's Day. There, you could find as fine an array of handkerchiefs and dresser scarves and perfumes as could be found anywhere in the world. There, fine perfumes like Evening in Paris and Radio Girl and anything by Coty and Revlon glistened and glimmered in pretty bottles. Penny candy and comic books were displayed as well as seasonal decorations. My mom still has glass beads and a small papier-mâché foil wreath I bought her for Christmas decorations with money I had earned with my county and state fair 4-H ribbons. The wreath, as I recall, cost a quarter, as did a small plastic Nativity scene Mama still brings out at Christmastime.

And always at Ben Franklin were the friendly lady clerks like Mildred, available to help with selections and sizes. They always seemed to know just when to ask if they could help and then would praise a little girl for her thoughtfulness and wisdom at getting such a nice gift for her mama. Mildred died a few years ago. But she worked at Ben Franklin long enough that not only had she helped me when I was a kid, but she also waited on my kids when they visited that wonderland during visits to their grandma.

The square of my hometown is largely vacant now. No longer are the streets clogged with cars on a Saturday afternoon and Saturday night. There is very little retail business performed any other time of the week either. Owners of once prosperous businesses retired or died and their stores with them. A bad economy forced the closing of others. With Ben Franklin, it might have been the economy, but as with others it was more likely a large discount chain in neighboring counties - I don't even have to mention the name of the firm, do I? - which knocked them out of competition. In my hometown, a person cannot find a pair of pants to buy or a pair of shoes. Unless it can be purchased at the local Hy-Vee grocery store or at Casey's convenience store, a consumer has to travel at least 25 miles, possibly 50, to buy what once was found in any of the several stores on the town square.

There were once half a dozen or more grocery stores, a meat locker, three dime stores, hardware stores, drug stores, appliance dealers, restaurants, a pool hall, taverns, jewelry stores, clothing and shoe stores, barber shops, a theater, and furniture stores on the square. Now the stores on the square offer more service places than retail; businesses include a tax preparation service, a flower and craft shop, tanning salon, an insurance agency, a couple of banks and a tavern.

Also a public library in the old Royal and lots of empty space.

Waterbed: It's Not Like Grandma's Feather Bed

We had been looking at waterbeds for a few months trying to decide if we really wanted one. Bob had heard from the Guys at Work, those authorities on all things to be considered, be it stir-frying cooking, movies, best buys in cars, stereos, or even family planning, that waterbeds were great for Bad Backs. And Bob has a Bad Back.

My friends, too, told me that we would like a waterbed. But many of my friends are of the younger or at least more liberal and progressive stripe. And besides, in the back of my mind I'd always sort of joined waterbeds to hallucinogenics or VW vans filled with pot-smoking, long-haired hippies listening to music played by swami-type oddballs with beards and 10-inch long fingernails. Waterbeds had never been quite respectable.

And then even our daughters got into the picture when one day Bob arrived home with daughter Bethany, who was quite young at the time, after a shopping trip where they'd stopped and looked at waterbeds.

"....And there was this beautiful bed, Mom, and it had a big mirror on the headboard and vases to put flowers and a real pretty top on it...What's that called? A canopy?....And oh, Mom, you would have loved it, it had a mirror under the canopy, a great big mirror! Wouldn't that be neat?"

"A mirror in the bed's canopy ceiling? Well, wouldn't that be handy?" I said to my innocent little daughter as I looked across at her dad who was keeping a straight face.

So it came about that we now have a waterbed. And not just any waterbed, either. No sir, it's a king-size waterbed, which in our average-size bedroom makes it appear as though we have wall-to-wall bed. There are farms in Third World countries smaller than our bed, that are capable of sustaining entire families. In fact, we had to move nearly everything else out of the room to accommodate the bed. It's not hardly decent.

There are double sets of storage drawers under the bed making it a tall piece of furniture and getting out of bed is roughly akin to crawling out of the back of a pickup full of oats.

I've had trouble becoming used to sleeping on a bed that moves around even though it contains those mysterious things called "baffles" which are supposed to cut down on wave motion. Even with those, however, I'm aware of more than normal movement when I turn over in bed, or when Bob rolls over because then I become the victim of a perceptible wave-swell. Also, I always seem to find myself in some kind of trough and have trouble when I'm half asleep and want to roll over or even get out of bed. I have to fight, scramble, claw and crawl around to, somehow or other, get out of the trough and send a kind of water-motion out so a wave will come back and give a boost out.

Bob felt this problem might be caused by not having enough water in the mattress, so he added more. It bulged up firmly and made sleeping on the waterbed somewhat similar to laying across the hood of a '53 Buick.

We were told by friends that it would take us about a month to become used to sleeping on the waterbed. I didn't know if I'd last that long.

I'll acquaint those who have decided to purchase a waterbed with some facts:

Your bed has been selected, purchased, brought home and put together in the manner of assembling a Tinker-Toy bridge. You fill the mattress with water and if the thing doesn't go through the floor - it'll weigh a ton, remember - you're pretty safe. If you're a chronic room-rearranger, as I am, you're out of luck. Where the bed is, it'll stay, probably forever. You may perhaps move a chair, a very small chair, from one corner to the other; that is, if you have any corners not filled with bed.

One other little-publicized problem of owning a waterbed is trying to purchase and fit bed linens for it. For a king-size bed, if you're lucky, you may be able to find sheets for less than $40. On sale. Then comes the task of putting the things on. First, though, you'll want to put on a mattress pad. They appear to be made from several layers of Kleenex or paper towel with maybe some sort of fiber such as wood shavings stirred in for good measure. A mattress pad resembles a disposable diaper, one of the cheaper, cheesier varieties. It has a band of elastic at each corner to help hold it on the vinyl mattress. Fitting one of these mattress pads on a waterbed takes the contortions and dexterity, I would imagine, of trying to put a jockstrap on a Sumo wrestler. You pull up a corner of the mattress, then hurry and slip the elastic strap around the heavy mattress before it drops or pulls you in and buries you.

Next, the sheets. With waterbed sheets, the bottom fitted sheet is sewn to the top sheet, so those who habitually pull the top sheet out from the bottom so their feet won't be "trapped," (I've heard this is a sign of and insecurity or at least I've tried to convince Bob of that for more than 30 years) will be out of luck. If they should try this little trick with waterbed sheets, they're liable to sprain something in their efforts.

Putting the fitted sheet on is somewhat like the mattress pad only besides the very real concern of becoming engulfed in the mattress, you also have to keep an eye on the mattress pad straps as you try to fit the sheet on. After the bed is neatly made and everything is tucked in and smoothed out and you're admiring your efforts, be aware that everything will come undone by approximately 1:30 a.m., if not before, and you'll be sleeping uneasily on vinyl and bunched-up sheets.

And if you're a lucky person such as I, your spouse will have selected a lovely bookcase headboard with a mirror right in the center, a nice sized mirror, too, with roses and daisies etched all around it. You will learn to never look in the mirror early in the morning. But sometimes you get sick and forget about the mirror and look in it anyway. You see a gray-green face with shadowed, baggy eyes, the kind my mom calls, "hollow-eyed," and your kids say in concern, "Are you going to need to go to the doctor, Mom?"

"Doctor?" I groan, "I don't need a doctor, I need an exorcist! Now leave me alone, please!" And they shove off the bed setting up a wave-like motion. Oh my.

Waterbeds are great. Or they are when you get used to them. All my friends said this was so.

But then they sometimes lie.

PC Strategy For 4-H

It was a very warm and humid afternoon when we visited the 1996 Iowa State Fair one day after we got off work. We had planned to make a whole evening of it and visit our favorite exhibits while we ate our way across the fairgrounds, sampling a little of this and a little of that.

My favorite exhibits at the fair can be found in the 4-H Building. I enjoy seeing the kids' projects, particularly the girls' sewing and needlecraft work. Bob likes to look at the guys' welding and carpentry projects and at photography exhibits.

As a former 4-Her, I know what kind of work it takes to get a project you've slaved over for weeks and months selected to go to the state fair. Tapped to be exhibited at the state fair, it's the best of the best. And because it is, I especially like to see what kind of awards the best of the best receive at the state fair.

I remember my own sewing projects selected by judges at our 4-H Achievement Day to be worthy to go to the Missouri State Fair. And I remember the thrill when I received blue ribbons for the projects. Above and beyond the monetary value - and a girl could acquire quite a nice little stack of change at both the state and county fairs earning awards, particularly blue ribbons - was the honor of getting a blue ribbon. Oh sure, a red or white ribbon would be OK, it was the state fair, after all. But a blue ribbon - first place among the best of the best? Well, there may be higher awards - the Congressional Medal of Honor, for instance - but they are few and far between. A blue ribbon reflected not only on the exhibitor and her family, but on the 4-H project leader and the whole club, and ultimately on the entire Putnam County 4-H organization.

At the 1996 Iowa State Fair we noticed a new ribbon attached to 4-H exhibits. It was a red, white and blue ribbon with a rosette at the top. We first noticed them on the outdoor exhibits of the farm machinery and welding projects. They must be some sort of grand prize, we thought at the time, transcending a blue ribbon. Then we went inside the exhibit building and I headed straight for the sewing exhibits. They, too, all had red, white and blue ribbons with the tri-color rosette at the top. There must be some explanation, I thought. Not everyone gets judged the same - not all of these projects were of the same caliber. In fact, I could see dresses and coats and suits which were superior to the quite good competition. So why did they all have the same awards?

I went to ask one of the 4-H officials and that is when I found out in this politically correct age, each project is getting the same award. It appears to be another attempt at making everyone feel good about themselves - the old enhanced self-esteem thing, don't you know.

They're dumbing down 4-H by awarding everyone the same prize!

Is nothing sacred anymore?

Ah, but I was told by the official that the kids who exhibited at the state fair would receive a comment sheet after the fair about their project with the judge writing how they had placed.

Big deal. One of the finer things about being the best of the best of the best is that everyone from competitors to grandpas and grandmas and proud parents can see it - a blue ribbon is public - not the same thing at all as a "comment sheet" received in the mail or attached to a returned fair exhibit to mull over in the family kitchen.

"If you're taking public comments about these new ribbons," I told the 4-H official, "Put me down on the side of: It stinks! It's not fair to the kids who do great work as opposed to good work, and you and I both know the difference." And I walked away and out of the People's Republic of 4-H Building. Frankly, my whole view of the fair was spoiled. Bob, too, although never in 4-H, concurred with my sentiments, and we soon decided we'd seen enough of the fair and headed for home.

I've since learned that 4-H is not the same organization it was when I was a kid. Then it was mostly for farm kids, but there were town-kid clubs, too, where we learned about public service, leadership, patriotism, faith, teamwork and practical living skills which have been carried on into adulthood by most of us. I still sew using many of the same tactics taught me at the kitchen table of a volunteer sewing leader, Delores Hudson, the mom of another 4-H member. My brother had woodworking projects and was taught by Virgil Anderson, a guy who was a self-employed carpenter - his sons were in our club, the Good Luck 4-H Club. Mary Emma Thompson, another 4-H mom, taught cooking skills. Among the things I learned from her was the correct way to make lemonade and how to garnish a drink glass attractively, using practical elements found in anyone's cabinet or flower garden.

Our 4-H leaders were volunteers and nearly all were either 4-H parents or 4-H grandparents.

Now, I find the philosophy of 4-H has changed and has become what sounds like a political arm of every liberal idea I have grown tired of having shoved down my throat, even down to spoiling my enjoyment of looking at 4-H kids' projects making it to the state fair.

The intellectual midgets who thought up this latest travesty - surprisingly this came from Iowa State University instead of the University of Iowa where you might expect this type of socialistic scheme would be spawned - should take to heart the words of the 4-H Pledge, which tens of thousands of us learned. "I pledge my heart to clearer thinking, my heart to greater loyalty, my hands to greater service and my health to better living for my club, my community and my country."

Nevertheless, those spoil-sports at Iowa State, who take themselves altogether too seriously, should take a good look at the pledge which has been so sadly overlooked in their social tinkering.

(And a few months later the strategists for political correctness in 4-H did exactly that and found they had second thoughts about the whole subject.)

Boys will be boys - Tim, Robbie and Mike.

Family Pet Horror Stories

Years ago when the kids were small, Bethany, who was six at the time, was missing her orange and white kitty, Cupcake. As she worried about Cupcake, I assured her that the cat had probably gone to the neighbors. Her brothers told her that in the past cats have wandered off to have kittens.

I really didn't think that was the case, but I let it go. I figured the cat might have gotten a fatal case of Dodge-fever and had been hit by a car or pickup.

A few days passed and the cat was dismissed from my mind, but only temporarily as it turned out.

Bethany's big brother decided one evening to go fishing since the ice had melted from the neighbor's pond - a place he hopes may contain king-sized bass. So off he went with the neighbor boy, the tackle box and his rod and reel. He wasn't gone very long, 20 minutes maybe, and upon his return he motioned for me to come into the kitchen away from his sisters. I began to be a little leery and was sure he was up to no good, especially as he came close to whisper his news in my ear.

"Hey, Mom, you know Bethany's cat that she's missing?" (I don't want to hear it, Tim!) "Well, I found it - guess where?" ("That's enough! I can about guess, just shut up before Bethany hears us.) He continued, "Remember last week when the ice on the pond was almost melted? Well, Bethany's cat must've been on that thin ice when he fell in, and it's real dead, but don't worry 'cause I got it out by using my rod and reel, hooking it and reeling it in - almost lost my lure, too."

I was getting concerned that Bethany might overhear the tale which was being related with all the delight and morbid gusto a male adolescent is capable of when acting as the bearer of bad news, particularly gross and revolting news. Eventually, though, he finally ran down.

As we were sitting down to supper that evening he seemed to be acting rather smug about his little sister's not knowing that her cat was no more - that he had traveled on to Cat Heaven. I decided to set him down a peg or two as he began eating his beef stew and complimented me on it, "Hey, Mom, this is pretty good, what kind of meat did you use?" I peered at him closely, looked over the tops of my glasses and replied ominously, "Take a guess!" as I motioned with my head across the road to the neighbor's pond.

Strangely, his appetite diminished and no more was ever said about the missing Cupcake.

I was relating this story to my neighbor, and as we laughed together over it she reminded me of a similar incident at our house a couple of years earlier - the time of the blizzard puppies.

We were in the middle of a treacherous sub-zero blizzard. The very pregnant dog which someone had dumped off in front of our place a couple weeks earlier had disappeared . The boys went out in the storm to look for her. They found her in the barn with her litter of newborn puppies. Getting a large box, they loaded all the pups in it and carried mama dog and the box of pups back to the house. The kids were heartbroken to discover that it was already too late for three of the puppies.

We placed the deceased pups outside to await a break in the weather and were left with five kids in various stages of sobs over the dead, or admiring oohs and ahs over the remaining puppies.

The next morning the snowstorm was over and the kids went outside to play. I lingered over my coffee dreading the thought of going outdoors. I looked out to where we'd put the dead puppies and sighed in relief when I saw they were gone, and mentally gave Bob a kiss for getting rid of them for me.

That afternoon as the sun brightly shined and the kids played outside, I heard a screech of horror and outrage from our youngest son, Robbie, who had been building a snow tunnel. He burst in the house and headed for his little sister, Jenny, who was four at the time. Just as his hands were about to reach her, I intervened to find out the cause of his very obvious distress.

By sorting out gasping, tearful sentences, I was able to discover the cause for his upset.

Bob hadn't disposed of the puppies as I'd assumed, after all. Innocent little Jenny had taken care of the matter all by herself by burying the puppies in a snowdrift, bless her heart. It wouldn't have been so bad if her brother hadn't chosen that same snowdrift to build his snow tunnel. And it was an unkind act of fate that he tunneled directly under (and in one case, directly into) Jenny's pet graveyard.

Following his story, Rob turned to me for consoling and comfort. I tried, I really tried, to keep a straight face, but soon gave up the pretense. I leaned back against the wall and slowly slid down and collapsed in laughter.

Sweat Bees And Blackberries

This year has provided a bumper crop of wild berries of every sort. First there were mulberries, then raspberries, Lately, there have been dewberries and blackberries. Only rarely do I pay any attention to wild berries, and I haven't gone near berry vines for years and years. That they're in season is only apparent to me by my car's windshield.

Like many of my likes and dislikes, I suppose my deep aversion to wild berries could be traced back to my childhood in the hills of north central Missouri, and some of the kid-traumas I experienced while growing up.

Among those experiences was the annual outing to pick wild blackberries for desserts and jelly-making. Berries appear to thrive best when the weather is as hot and humid as it is likely to be in mid-July, and it was generally the hottest, stickiest day of the year when my mom would say, "We're going blackberry picking today!" That meant, even in the heat, a person would be required to wear a long-sleeved shirt and long pants and (groan) shoes to avoid brambles and briars. My aunt, Virginia, and my cousins across the field would also accompany us and I always knew how the day would turn out before it even began. My brother would have a temper fit and sit on the ground and refuse to do anything. Cousin Sue and I would be together, being the same age and nearly best friends, even if we were kin. Her younger sister, Sandy, would probably pout and whine all the time, and little Joe Dean would either be cute and have to be carried, or cry and have to be carried.

Berry vines tore at my flesh and there were always snakes close to berry patches, big, well-fed snakes. And the very best berry patches always seemed to be in the middle of a pasture containing a bull, a big mean bull.

Mosquitoes, chiggers, ticks and most especially, sweat bees were rampant, and always somewhere hidden from view would be my old enemy, poison ivy.

I have fond memories of my childhood, but blackberry-picking time is not one of them.

Several years ago, though, when our sons were just little boys, I decided to take them berry picking and what better place than one of the many wild places near our home in the foothills of south Warren County? My neighbor across the road was going, too, along with her two little boys. We decided, based on my childhood experiences, not to go any place real overgrown, merely to the fence rows of a nicely chewed-down pasture at another neighbor's. We'd avoid much of the grief-causing, armpit-high weeds and brush patches we would otherwise find ourselves in.

We weren't dressed real appropriately; I had on cut-off jeans and a skimpy halter-top with one of Bob's old, long-sleeved shirts left unbuttoned. My friend was dressed about the same.

It was a beautiful morning with a nice breeze blowing as we picked berries, chatted and kept an eye on the little boys. All of a sudden came the sound of a kid screaming - one of mine, and the rest of the little boys were exclaiming or crying in fear or sympathy or both.

We dropped our buckets and ran to find that my Robbie, who was around three, had fallen over a barbed wire fence and caught his arm on the barbs, ripping a long, deep gash in his poor little fatty upper arm. I felt sick and my legs began shaking as I thought of our predicament: two half-clad women, five kids under the age of six, at least half a mile or more from the car, then through stock gates and field tracks just to get to the gravel road.

I took off my old, sweaty shirt and tied a sleeve around Robbie's arm to try to stop some of the bleeding. Running and carrying him, while dragging along his brother, with another brother trying to keep up and my neighbor doing the same with her boys, we ran to the car, bounced over ruts and somehow or other got 20 miles to the doctor where Robbie had his arm stitched up. I had to turn my head away to avoid seeing the needle go in my little boy's tender skin, and realized for the first time how indecently dressed I was. I shudder to even think of that day.

And that's the last time I went berry picking.

At least until last week when the girls came running excitedly to me with their hands full of large purple berries. "Will you go berry picking with us, Mom?" they asked. I've learned that saying no to an activity like this to two little girls is never easy or simple, so as usual and against my better judgment, I yielded.

It was one of those magical, breezy summer, late afternoons as we rode our bikes a mile or so away. We picked berries as I told them of berry-picking expeditions when I was a kid and other family stories as I thought of them, like the ill-fated trek the time Rob ripped open his arm. "Oooooo," they said, "Were you scared?" We watched pretty birds, too, and smelled the nice smells found in the countryside - of wildflowers and the loamy, leafy smell of a nearby creek bottom.

I found a nice-sized wild grapevine hanging near a ditch. I looked at it a while with a strange thought going through my mind, then impulsively decided to see if grapevines were as much fun as they used to be. As my little girls stood nearby, watching in open-mouthed amazement, their approaching-middle-age mom let out a Tarzan yell and swooped down and over the deep ditch swinging on the grapevine. Then they tried it.

Soon it was time to head home with the berries we'd picked. We were tired and sweaty, itchy and mud-smeared. But that was OK.

We had just created a memory.

A PC Bible? Holy Cow!

I see there's a new Bible out. The King James version has obviously become passé and not hip enough for some folks. This new one is in contemporary jargon, more so apparently than the Revised Standard or other similar Bible editions that have already done away with the thees and thous. Now we won't even have to wonder to which gender we're directing prayers or to whom we're just speaking to as a friend or a comforter. God is now gender non-specific. God is now known as Mother/Father.

God has become an It!

The new Bible is so politically correct, there is no reference to "dark." No, that might be interpreted to be a racial remark. Now it is "without light." No longer are there the lame and the halt, the blind or crippled. Those words are considered insensitive and aren't used.

In fact, The Des Moines Sunday Register in an editorial about the new Bible stated that "God is generally viewed" as having no gender. Excuse me? Generally viewed by whom? Where are these people who "generally view" God to be Mother/Father? I have yet to find anyone who thinks of God as an It.

I'm not a biblical scholar, God knows. Probably the deepest I ever studied the Bible was in Vacation Bible School and going to Sunday School every Sunday morning as a kid to learn memory verses and Bible stories. To me, God has always been male, and I admit it, a white male. God has long white hair and a white beard and wears a flowing white gown. Jesus, another white male, has long brown hair and a brown beard, also kindly dark brown eyes. Those were the illustrations I saw in my Sunday School quarterlies or in my Bible during Sunday morning sermons as I suffered through long sermons while trying not to fidget. This was back in a time when fidgeting during Sunday morning church service was looked upon as rude and disrespectful and was frowned upon - severely frowned upon by parents and grandparents.

The King James Bible has always appealed to me, possibly because I am a traditionalist and also because I enjoy the lyrical, poetic and often mystical quality of writing. It somehow seems more "biblical," even though I realize it was penned centuries ago by clerics and scholars in a time when the majority of people were illiterate, let alone possessed anything remotely akin to a book, even the Holy Bible.

My sentiments have been passed on to my children, I suppose. I remember a couple of years ago when my daughter, Jenny, was involved in a community Christmas program. She was to read a portion of the Christmas story in a newer, trendier version of St. Matthew. She was 17, and stumbled over the word, "intercourse," and refused to speak the phrase when it came to the part of the story where Mary and Joseph did not "know" each other until after Jesus was born. Jenny went with the old version rather than the newer, coarser version. I'll admit I was proud of her for that.

I was raised in a Southern Baptist church in Missouri. In Missouri,

Southern Baptist churches are numerous. More like what Methodists are in Iowa and Lutherans are in Minnesota. Southern Baptists have slowly arrived in Iowa, which is even now probably considered a mission field.

I remember the time a few years ago when I sat beside my mom in my hometown church and there was some mention during the morning announcements of sending a donation to a mission field. I assumed they were talking about sending blankets, medical supplies or Bibles to Russia or Africa. Imagine my surprise when I heard the donation was to be directed to Storm Lake, Iowa.

The Southern Baptist denomination is the largest Protestant denomination in the United States and is growing, as are other conservative evangelical denominations. There might be a good reason for that in that they do not embrace every new social anomaly such as a Bible where God is an It. Trendy new beliefs, theories and lifestyles are not automatically embraced or accepted as the norm, or even good. Quite the opposite. And the entire Bible is interpreted as true, not bits and parts of it, with this part being a fairy tale and another part being *fairly* accurate based on historical accounts of a documented event. I was raised believing all of the Bible is true.

And I know this is a fact because Katie Matthews, a sweet little round white-haired woman, told me so when I was about five. She was my Sunday School teacher and was probably one of the most influential people in my life.

Generally speaking, preaching is not my thing. And for that matter, that's not what I'm doing now. It's just that somebody has to take a public stand - and this forum is as good as any - to say, "Whoa! This new Bible-thing, where God is an It, is horrible and stupid and tasteless and borders on blasphemy."

Just because people with too much time on their hands want to rewrite and change something that has inspired millions for centuries, does that make it good?

I think it's about time those scholars contemplate something besides their navels, and return to the business at hand of helping mankind - beginning with themselves - the way the traditional Bible advised, instead of being politically correct, even down to changing God to an It.

Medical Scare

I paid a visit to my doctor not long ago and was given welcome news.

"Well, you don't have cancer," he said.

I slumped in relief. That had been a very real fear hovering over me since a routine physical last February revealed I had abnormal cells.

In the past, my physicals had always gone two ways. Either I was healthy and pregnant, or I was healthy, but it wouldn't hurt me to lose a few pounds. I'm not accustomed to hearing anything bad or frightening.

A week after my physical, accompanied by tests which awaited lab results, I had dropped into the office of the Record-Herald, something I do each week. I called my daughters at home to tell them I would be there within the hour.

"Mom," Jenny said, "The clinic called and you're supposed to call them back."

I had my first twinge of foreboding right then. Usually after a physical, doctors and clinics want nothing from me except my prompt payment.

I called the clinic immediately and was given the news. A report had come back from the lab on one of my tests, a pap smear, showing a "level three."

"A level three-what?" I asked, while trying to keep my voice from shaking. "Explain a level three to me and what it means."

Well, there are four levels of results on this particular test, I was told. A level-one means the results are normal; a level-four is cancer.

My test results showed level-three, which revealed abnormal cells, a pre-cancer condition. But it wasn't anything to get too worried about, I was told.

Not get worried? Worried? I wasn't worried, I was terrified!

There's not a heckuva lot of difference between the numbers three and four, I thought, and the term for my disorder, "dysplasia" sounded alarming.

Should I come in to see the doctor now? I asked. Well, no, I was told, because it was nearly five o'clock. They would set me up an appointment with a specialist in Des Moines. "For tomorrow?" I asked. Well no, I was told, I couldn't get in to see the specialist for three weeks, and then only that early because the doctor had received a cancellation.

"Who canceled?" I asked wearily. "Some woman who just died of cervical cancer?"

The next day I could think of nothing else but the phone call from the clinic. And the term "abnormal cells" would not leave my mind. My imagination ran wild, as well as my fears. Bob was worried, too, and wanted something done right then. Why wait around? he asked. Why indeed?

We didn't say anything to the kids, but the girls are nosy and have keen senses of hearing, as well as finely tuned senses of something-being-in-the-wind. They put two and two together and began asking about me as I dodged their questions and tried not to be abrupt with them as I'm likely to do when I'm worried or frightened. And what scared me even more is they were extra considerate of me and went out of their way to be cooperative and helped me with housework without being told to. It wasn't natural.

Another day passed, and finally in desperation I called the clinic back. "I can't stand this waiting for an appointment three weeks away," I said, and then tried a half-hearted joke, "I'm supposed to be thinking of amusing things to write in a weekly column to entertain winter-weary readers and all I can think about is if I'll live to see another year."

My plea wouldn't get me in to see another doctor any more quickly, they explained, because they didn't like to deal with any other doctor except this particular specialist to which I was being referred.

I caved in and called Bob at work, crying and afraid. I knew I'd gain his ear. After his experiences with medical specialists - as many as 15 at once, according to their bills - dealing with his parents before they passed away, with a few exceptions, he has no great love or trust for the profession.

Find a different doctor, he said, after talking with the guys at work about my abnormal cells. They had all compared gynecological notes, I later learned, given all their experience with wives or girlfriends. I cringed at the idea of my body parts being discussed between the guys I'll later be seeing at office gatherings.

On that cold, cheerless February afternoon after making several phone calls, I was given the name of a specialist in Des Moines who came highly recommended by a person whose opinion I trusted.

I called and explained my dilemma, and they seemed to understand my unstated fears.

Yes, I was told, the doctor can see you....(When, I wondered hopefully, next week?)...Um, how about tomorrow afternoon?

And so the first of several visits was carried out. However, learning about my abnormal cells did not happen quickly, I found.

It took nearly seven months to find out, with no doubts, that I didn't have cancer. It took one embarrassing and intimate test after another with accompanying lab work to finally receive a report of NORMAL cell structure.

Oh, I could go into quite lengthy detail about some of the tests - like going into an examining room wearing a backless paper gown and followed by a big cylinder of nitrogen, knowing that some procedure involving it and parts of me was about to be performed.

The specialist had explained early-on that level-three test results had varying degrees from not-bad-at-all to prepare-for-the-worst. Somehow that message had never reached me when I was first warned that I had level-three abnormal cells.

I felt less terminal than I had previously; except for my tonsils and appendix, I still had all my parts and wanted to keep them. Nevertheless, I continued to worry until the recent welcome news from the doctor.

There's an advertising slogan for - of all things - an automotive supply company, which I heartily endorse where my body is concerned: "There are NO unimportant parts."

I consider all my parts important.

The Burden Laid Aside By Churches

I was halfway listening to the news on the radio on the drive with Bob to work one morning when something caught my attention.

"What was that?" I asked him, "Something about churches providing services that the government is cutting back on? Did I hear right?"

He assured me I did, and we both agreed right then this was a trend that should continue, and perhaps be enhanced.

Imagine what would happen if all the churches in our land would actually perform the services they were ordained to do in the first place? That is, provide spiritual strength and succor to all who asked for or needed it, to help the afflicted, the hungry, the poor, the ill, the lame and the halt. And maybe the churches and their servants could even act as role models to parents, kids, civic and government leaders, educators, entertainers and yes, even columnists.

What a better world we would have.

That's more or less the way I remember it used to be when I was a kid attending the First Baptist Church of Unionville, a Southern Baptist congregation, and members provided help to less fortunate people in the community.

That was back in the days of the 1950s and early '60s when it was an acknowledged fact that some people were poor, but in order to not be poor, or at least to survive, one had to work, and sometimes work very, very hard.

Nothing much like today when it appears that all citizens - and noncitizens, as well - have a constitutional right to have government housing with central heat, food on the table containing all the correct nutrients, as well as the right to stay at home and not work for a living because, by golly, pride and honor and self-respect be damned, a person makes less at minimum wage than on welfare, so why work? Or so it has been for more than 30 years.

Back when I was a kid, and when Lyndon Johnson and his Great Society were still in Texas, or at least not in the White House, churches and their members looked after the less fortunate in our community. It was expected. It was duty.

Ours was a one-parent household - Daddy was in a VA hospital. Our mother raised my brother and me on a small 19-acre, not-particularly-prosperous farm in Missouri. We would be considered victims of poverty today, but we weren't then. We were poor, not REAL poor, but just plain poor. But then, so were a lot of others, to tell the truth. And we attended and were members of the Baptist church.

The only thing really hard-up families received in the guise of welfare was coal. They received assistance in heating their homes, often little more than shacks, in the winter and that is about it as far as I know. The local churches assisted poor people with food and clothing whether they were disabled veterans, or poor elderly people or down-on-their-luck poor families with children.

A lot of my clothing had first been handed down to me by older cousins or other girls in our church. Some of my outfits were made by my mom. When I outgrew them, my clothes were saved as were my brother's, and distributed to families with kids who could wear them.

Every Saturday, we stopped in town at the home of a large poor family, and brought them a gallon jar of fresh milk; we would pick up the clean gallon jar from the week before, and bring it back full the next Saturday. Garden produce and other stuff grown on the farms which so many of us then lived on were also shared with them and with others.

And throughout Putnam County, countless families from other churches were looking after their less fortunate brothers and sisters. That's part of what church was all about. We were taught to help others from Sunday School lessons right on to the message in the morning sermon.

And if poor families worked hard at whatever they could turn their hands to, they were not thought less of for needing help. They were at least trying, was the generally held opinion, and nobody can do more than try. And most of the people I remember as being dirt-poor eventually made it out of it, got their families raised, and moved up in life, as did their kids.

That's the way it used to be.

Somewhere along the line things got a little out of whack when the government walked in and took over good works, and as is usual with anything the government gets involved in, things became generally screwed up. We've had generations who feel it is their right to have everything handed to them by the government and the being-bled-dry, tax-paying public: Clothing, food, housing, fuel, medical care, but not work, oh my no. Not work.

And churches, having to no longer look after and worry over the less fortunate in their communities turned to other things: Fund-raising for every fringe group outside the U.S. and sometimes inside it, politicking, lobbying, picketing, and just generally - pardon the expression - raising hell on every contemporary issue under the sun, and many times unaware of a need for their services and spiritual help right in their own back yards.

The religious leaders, the preachers and priests, began making the news, too. Other concerns came into play. By not having so much to do in leading and directing their flocks in charitable work, they sometimes turned to drum-beating, navel contemplating and to wine, women and song, and at times, drugs; and more often than I like to think, to little boys and girls.

And it was with these thoughts in mind upon hearing the report that churches might begin to pick up where government services are being dropped, I thought: No, they aren't taking over services from the government.

They are merely picking up a burden and an obligation that has been laid aside for too long.

A Plague Of Counselors

I sometimes wonder how today's kids are going to turn out. They're viewed by many as whiny, pampered, overindulged, overweight, spoiled, lazy, grasping, non-productive slackers. Blame is placed on parents, the school system, rap singers, broken families, working mothers and peer pressure.

Another theory I'm leaning toward might be that many kids are turning into wienies by being counseled half to death to make them feel good or to enhance their self-esteem. Instead of being trusted to deal with whatever upsetting thing is currently in their lives, kids are being "counseled," oftentimes uninvited and unwelcome.

Following Hurricane Andrew a few years ago, counselors were brought into Florida to help the children. Families were having trouble getting food or water or shelter, but by golly, there were plenty of counselors. I heard one say that such action was warranted because the kids had witnessed this storm and many didn't have their toys. Toys? I wonder how kids in a place like, say, Sarajevo, manage to cope?

In Florida, instead of giving the kids some rakes and shovels, along with a hug and a pat on the back, and sending them out to help clean up storm debris if for no other reason than to give them something do besides worry or feel sorry for themselves, they had counselors.

Nearer home, in a small Iowa town, a dog got out of its pen and bit four kids. The dog was later shot by a deputy sheriff. The news report said a counselor "was kept busy all day dealing with students who witnessed the attacks or saw the dog killed."

OK. So the kids might have been a little upset. But think about it. How many of those same kids have calmly watched people be vaporized, burned to death, disemboweled, chain-sawed, hacked, stabbed, shot, drowned or savaged by large, white sharks in the movies and on television, including the evening news?

Last year, Des Moines police arrested a suburban cop, who along with being with a woman not his wife in the wee hours of the morning, was also in possession of several thousand dollars worth of methamphetamines and pornographic materials. Among the porn-stuff were videotapes where the cop played the starring role - former cop, I might add, since he was soon fired. Perhaps more startling than this to many folks was the fact that the guy was arrested while still attached to a battery-operated (ahem!) personal appliance. And shocking to many, who as teenagers wouldn't think of so much as even trying to make out in the family sedan, the cop with the drugs, the porn, the sex toy and the strange woman, was driving his mom's van. Besides being a law enforcement officer, he also worked with school kids in DARE (Drug Abuse Resistance Education) programs and was an athletic coach. All in all and by all reports, a fine upstanding family man to be commended for community service. That is, until his arrest.

A couple of weeks after this news broke, came more news from the suburbs. It seems that an eighth grade teacher there, an attractive young woman in her 20s, married and a mother, had allegedly been carrying on with a young man for a couple of years. The kid had been 14 when he and the teacher began their entanglement. His parents filed charges against the young woman - the kid was by then 16 - and last week she pleaded guilty to charges of third-degree sex abuse.

These news reports caused quite a stir in central Iowa and in the midst of the usual water-cooler gossip, warped humor and chit-chat, there was much agonizing on the effect the incidents would have on the kids. Indeed, counselors were called in to help the suburban school kids deal with their feelings about all of it. Considering what some kids put up with these days outside the clutches of counselors, a dopehead cop with dirty movies and a sex gadget, or an affair between an older woman teacher and a teen-age boy is pretty tame stuff.

There are many competent, maybe even gifted, counselors, and in some cases their help may be needed or wanted. But there are also counselors who are self-serving incumbents of a job that to many is murky at best, suspicious and probably harmful at worst, and who perpetuate the need for their services; job security it's called.

Counselors have become pacifiers, it seems, and any time something beyond the everyday occurs, their help is sought to help kids get through it. Get through what, life?

We had counselors when I was in school, but our best counselors were our friends, a coach or a favorite and trusted teacher. Mostly though, talking out things with friends was the best help a troubled or worried or frightened kid could get. And that is pretty much the way it is today, except today there is more of a push to use counselors, some of whom, to be candid, have problems of their own.

I find many in agreement with this view. "We're bringing up kids in an atmosphere where they don't have to cope with anything," said one guy. "There's always someone near to take care of things for them. And we wonder why so many can't cope with marriage, jobs, raising kids or even small details of being on their own!" he huffed. Others tell me counseling is necessary today. "Things are different than when you were a kid, Linda," I'm told. Oh really?

Spare me. No, things aren't much different today than when I was a kid, feelings-wise. We didn't have AIDS or drugs to cope with or visual and graphic, constitutionally-protected pornography, violence and sex in movies and TV. "Andy Griffith," and "My Three Sons," are a long way from Madonna's "Truth or Dare," or "Married....With Children." We had Art Linkletter, not Howard Stern. But we had our times.

I was 10 and my brother was 8 when the sheriff came to get our mentally ill dad and take him to the state mental hospital. Events leading up to that were not pleasant, believe me. Who consoled, advised and counseled my brother and me for what we saw and heard? No professional, that's for sure. We kids were helped by each other and friends and relatives.

As teenagers we witnessed the aftermath of a passenger jet crash, which killed all on board. The plane or parts of it plowed into the field near the home of our friends. For a couple of weeks afterward as soldiers were brought in from Fort Leonard Wood to guard the crash site, our school bus would pass the local Ford garage where bodies were being brought to the temporary morgue there. We heard from our friends living near the crash site of the gory scenes they came upon; of bodies and parts of them in trees, brush or still strapped in seats and nearly buried in the ground.

But we didn't get counseling. We talked among ourselves.

When the dad of a classmate was brutally murdered, we consoled our friend, and attended his dad's funeral. And we talked it out among ourselves. There were other murders, suicides, fatal accidents and tragedies which occur in communities where everyone usually knows everyone else. But we handled our feelings, our worry and grief ourselves. I don't feel we're worse off because of it either; quite the contrary.

Yes, kids of the '50s and 60s had their share of emotional troubles and woes, not the least of which was the specter of The Bomb hovering over our heads and the assassination of our young, heroic, handsome president. But counseling didn't intrude in our lives, not did we seek it out or even consider such a thing.

We took care of our worries and problems and traumas through the very best resources: Talking it over with our friends, working through it by ourselves, or secret and silent prayer - admitting to praying was not considered terribly cool, even then.

And you know something? Those things are still best.

The author and her life-long counselor, her mother.

A Two Cow Dairy Herd

It began as most of my stories do, by a chance remark from one of my kids.

The girls and I were headed home from the city when Bethany noticed a large dairy herd gathered under a grove of shade trees. "Those cows sure are pretty," she said, "What kind are they?"

I told her they were Holsteins and thought to be the very best breed of milk cows.

"Are they the kind you had when you were a little girl and had milk cows?" she asked.

I laughed. No, they weren't the kind we had.

And then as often happens, a story evolved as I began remembering out loud and told my daughters about milk cows.

When I was growing up in the hills of Missouri, nearly every farm family had milk cows - nothing so grand as a dairy herd, but at least one milk cow.

We had two, Spot and Wienie, and they were milked by hand. The cows were nearly considered members of the family. Each had her own personality and peculiarity. They were the same breeds as nearly everyone else's in our neighborhood, Jersey and Guernsey. Families then weren't so partial to one particular breed as they are now; they bought what was available and affordable at a farm auction or the weekly livestock auction. Few were purebred. My Uncle Kenneth, for instance, had a milk cow that was oddly marked - it was a brindle cow, and was a very mixed breed. My grandparents' milk cows were also mixed breeds. I remember at least one black white-face cow, which isn't even known to be a milker. But my grandpa wasn't partial to milk cows anyway, his interest lay in fine beef cattle, and the only breed worthy of the name, in his opinion, was Black Angus.

Spot and Wienie had received their names from the fact that Spot, a wide-hipped Jersey, had white spots. Wienie was a more narrow-hipped version of Spot and received her name because her udders were nicely shaped to fit a person's hand and resembled wienies. Spot's udders, on the other hand, were large, fat and badly scarred due to her fondness for going through fences. She was hard to milk and it would take so long to get the job done she'd begin to lose patience and in all likelihood, try to knock over the bucket of milk.

We didn't have a dairy barn, nor really much of a barn at all; it was more like a shed and wasn't used very much. When Spot and Wienie came up to the barn lot to be milked, if the weather was halfway decent at all, they were milked where they stood beneath the maple trees with chickens peacefully scratching around and pecking nearby.

I remember the sound of milk pinging in the bottom of an empty galvanized milk bucket and the thicker, foamy sound of it as the bucket filled. I remember the smell of the cow as I leaned my forehead into her flank, and the smell of fresh, warm milk as I worked, occasionally squirting a stream of milk into the gaping mouths of nearby begging kitties. I laughed when it'd hit them in the face causing them to have to work to get it washed off.

And who can ever forget the stinging sensation of a cow tail being flipped across the face as the cow attempted to switch away flies or just did it to be rascally. I always dreaded the feel of her tensing and gathering her muscles to lift her leg and shift around. Or kick the bucket. In any case it meant moving quickly to prevent the disaster of tipping over the bucket of milk, losing my balance on the milking stool, or getting stepped on.

Spot and Wienie gave milk not particularly noteworthy for the volume or butterfat content, but enough for our needs and some milk and cream to sell to the produce man.

The milk we got every morning and every evening was first strained through filters to remove any impurities such as dirt, hair or bugs that had dropped into it. Then it was poured into a cream separator, a machine that separated the milk from the cream.

I still remember when we got the separator, almost certainly from someone's farm auction. Before that we would have to let the milk set until the cream rose to the surface and then skim off the cream. With a separator we didn't have to do that.

I grew up on the dairy products that were provided by Spot and Wienie. I doubt if I tasted margarine until I was 16 because with some of the cream we got, we made our own butter. That was a Saturday morning chore my brother and I took turns doing. Neither of us liked the job. Using a butter churn - not the old-fashioned wooden dasher type, I'm not THAT old! - we'd churn and churn and churn until an ache developed between the shoulder blades and a kid was just about sure an arm was going to fall off. "Is it about done yet?" we whined, knowing good and well it wasn't. One of the best sounds to hear then was that of soft globs of butter beginning to form as the buttermilk separated and made a sloshing noise against the inside of the glass churn.

To this day I have scant interest in antiques such as butter churns that are used as decorative clutter in trendy restaurants or to decorate mantels or curio shelves in many homes. What is a charming remnant of yesteryear to others reminds me of a hated chore and a stiff arm.

But you couldn't beat the taste of homemade butter melting into freshly-baked hot rolls.

My mom made the best cottage cheese around as far as I was concerned. Cottage cheese was made by allowing a large pan of milk to sour until it "clabbered." Then it was slowly heated while more chunks of clabber formed. Pouring the stuff into a colander, the watery whey was drained off and the remaining curds were rinsed off with cold water.

To make really excellent cottage cheese, my mom then mixed cream, salt and pepper into it. And it tasted SO GOOD. I never got tired of it.

Some of my mom's friends put sugar on their cottage cheese and made it sweet. I hated that and viewed their offerings about the same as I viewed people who actually put sugar on sliced tomatoes! Both unnatural acts, I thought then. And still do.

The cottage cheese was so good and different from commercially-made cottage cheese....well, there is no comparison, and it took me many years to acquire a taste for the other kind, since it tasted squishy, bland and pasty.

Milk and cream, and always plenty of it, is what I remember about dairy products when I was a kid. Our milk, skim milk it's called now; "ol' blue john," my mom called it, always was kept in the refrigerator in Hi-C cans with the tops cut out. We didn't have such a thing as Tupperware or Rubbermaid containers - I suspect my mom was one of the first to latch onto the idea of recycling anything she could. Only it wasn't recycling then, it was "making do." The milk to be sold was kept in large galvanized milk cans in the cool dark depths of the cellar.

We had milk at every meal, fresh cream on cereal and over fruit; and whipped cream - REAL whipped cream unlike the stuff you get when using what's referred today as "whipping cream." We also used it for homemade ice cream without having to go to the grocery store and lay out $15 for supplies.

As my story to my daughters about milk cows ran down, we passed a sign announcing it was June, the dairy month.

Somehow it seemed the perfect ending.

Dangers For Children In The 90s

Our son Robbie, who was 20 at the time, was planning a trip to Chicago to visit a friend; he was going to be driving a car that, at best, was not particularly dependable. His dad and I reminded him of that, but no amount of unpleasant or discouraging words on our part would sway Rob from his planned trip. I might add that his Chicago friend was of the feminine gender, the heart was involved and any common sense - and that particular commodity has always been on the meager side in this child of mine - had flown out the window.

Parental warnings went out from his dad: "OK then, go to Chicago if you feel you've got to, but if and when your car breaks down on the interstate, don't be calling home for me to come and pick you up." (I heard those stern words and immediately spotted a lie.)

Rob heatedly assured his male parent that's the last thing in the world he would do; he would crawl home first, (or more realistically, call his older brother who lives midway between Chicago and Des Moines) and besides, he'd been working on his car and had added a little of this and a little of that and it "should hold together" on the long drive.

His dad had delivered his warning. I, as his mother, gave him a warning of my own. My warning was somber and more terse: "You can remember what your dad said, but if you should break down or have an accident, you call home anyway. There are evil people just waiting around for someone like you to need help on the interstate. They're just waiting out there. Now unless you want to take a chance on your head showing up on the shelf of someone's refrigerator, or your parts getting pickled or winding up in the meat-keeper of some sick creep's deep freeze, you'll remember what I said. Be careful."

"Yeah. Right," he grimaced, "You know that's pretty gross, Mom."

Yes, it was gross all right. But very effective.

He didn't change his mind about the trip to Chicago, but he did go back to his car, double check everything, and kept a tire iron handy. I had gotten him so spooked and jacked up that even a Good Samaritan would've had trouble approaching Robbie if he would have needed help.

Oh, and one more thing. He soon bought a new car, taking no chances on his old car breaking down anywhere. And the friend he was so fired up to visit in Chicago? She became his bride.

A recent episode occurred similar to my warning to Robbie, only to his younger teen-aged sister, Jenny. She, too, was hitting the road, only near our home and on her bicycle.

She came home one afternoon, scarlet-faced, perspiring, huffing and puffing and worn out.

She had been riding her bike on the nearby highway, she said, and remembered my warning about staying off the road as sunset approaches. "With people driving west, the sun's in their eyes and they might miss seeing a kid on a bicycle," I'd warned my kids time and again.

Jenny decided she'd leave her bike hidden in some weeds and come home by way of walking through the neighbor's cornfield, then crossing to our place.

"And then, Mom, I got in the middle of the cornfield, and it was so tall I couldn't tell where I was. I couldn't even see our barn! I THOUGHT I was headed in the right direction, but I remembered the stories you've told us about kids getting lost in cornfields....and there were gopher mounds and holes all over the place and I just KNEW I'd fall in one and break my ankle and nobody would know where I was.

"And then I started worrying about old wells. I thought 'What if one of these gopher holes is really an old well?' And I remembered all the stories you've told us about old wells being in the middle of nowhere and nobody knew it until someone fell in....

"I sure am glad to be home," she sighed in relief.

Apparently, I've done a good job of warning my kids on some of the pitfalls and dangers they could encounter if not careful. Now if they will just remember some of the warnings without becoming too frightened to enjoy life.

When I was a kid, my mother's warnings to me included: Don't swim right after I've eaten. Don't run with a stick or I'd poke out my eye. Don't walk on thin ice. Don't swim without a buddy, and stay away from dirty pond water because it might cause polio.

She would probably disagree, but I really think she had fewer things to warn me and my brother about than I've had for my children.

When I was a kid we had real hazards, but only vague, phantom boogiemen.

Today, the boogiemen have become real-life monsters.

Shabby Treatment In Nation's Capital

It was ironic that on the very week in 1986 our nation was celebrating the bicentennial of the U.S. Constitution, I would be in Washington, D.C., feeling for all the world that the inalienable rights and liberties our Constitution guarantees me were being threatened.

I had accompanied a group of farm women to D.C. to visit Iowa members of Congress to share with them concerns and opinions from "back home." But in all the rounds of visits and just plain gawking around at the most powerful place in the country, a place that has seen and heard so much history, we were made to feel like criminals, or at the very least, undesirables.

Every government building we visited resembled an armed camp with dozens of uniformed, armed police officers around. Large concrete, dirt-filled urns blocked drives and walks making driving or walking in and around Capitol Hill more like a maze. Each time we entered a building our belongings were searched and we had to walk through metal detectors. It was that way everywhere with varying degrees of thoroughness, but most especially I felt the surveillance, the creepy feeling of sliminess, the pervading aura of suspicion, the sense that we must be guilty of something to be treated in the shabby way we were - I felt it most acutely in the Capitol Building. I was not alone in my sentiments of being treated in a contemptible way, as others voiced the same concerns.

We entered the Capitol to sit in on a session of the Senate, thanks to the gallery passes we had from Sen. Charles Grassley. We entered the east side of the Capitol and I was awed by its size, the paintings, statues, murals - everything about it. The first thing our group faced once inside the building had been the usual search of our purses along with going through the metal detection device. We went upstairs to the Senate and were faced with a couple of young men demanding our cameras. Yes, I'd read the rules of etiquette on the back of my gallery pass. When it said no picture-taking, I'd put my camera away in my purse. I could say the cameras were taken or were asked for, but those verbs are too tame.

Seized, I think, would be a more accurate term; seized by a couple of smug, young preppies about the age of my oldest son, I suppose. Abrupt, crass, rude, power-mad little creeps who appeared to think that security clearance badges worn around their thick necks gave them a considerable amount of clout.

We handed over our cameras and traveled on to the Senate chamber, the glow diminishing from our expectations of witnessing democracy at work. But wait! We had another search to submit to. Our purses and other belongings were gone through again and the security officer asked if any of us had anything with batteries. A lady in front of our group held up her checkbook with one of those little calculators on it. She was told to leave the line and return only after she'd checked the calculator back at a cloak room. I asked the officer what the deal with batteries was. "They can be used as detonation devices," he said chillingly. Luckily, nobody in our group had pace makers or hearing aids with batteries. God knows what would have become of them.

Finally, after once again going through a metal detector we were allowed to go into the Senate chamber and sit in the gallery. All this we'd gone through just to see a nearly empty Senate with Sen. Proxmire speaking on the Strategic Defense Initiative (more commonly known as Star Wars) to a C-Span TV camera. The only others there besides a stenographer, were Sen. Byrd and a couple of others I didn't recognize in a three-man huddle appearing to be enjoying a good joke. I took a piece of scrap paper from my purse to jot down a couple of notes and was suddenly pounced on when my shoulder was grabbed by a self-important young woman - a female twin of the guys who had my camera - who jabbed her finger in my face and hissed, "No note taking!" I put my pen and paper scrap away, simmering all the time and we left the gallery shortly afterward. I gave the young woman a look that told her I suspected she had capped teeth, wore falsies and dingy underwear and possessed the morals of a mink.

I don't know who these people are with the security clearance badges, whether they're regular civil servants, or Senate pages or aides. But in nearly every instance we were greeted with discourtesy, abruptness, contempt and disdain. We felt favored if were met with mere ho-hum indifference or boredom. The only places we felt comfortable were in the offices of Sen. Grassley and our own Fifth District Congressman Lightfoot, both Iowans, and with staff members who smiled and didn't ask to look through our belongings. I could appreciate the emotions of refugees in hostile areas abroad who sought asylum in U.S. embassies. Only I was an Iowan in a foreign environment, my nation's capitol of all places, seeking asylum and reassurance if only through a friendly greeting in our politicians' offices. My God.

The whole experience of that one day on The Hill kind of threw a shadow on the rest of my visit to Washington. I acknowledge the fact that I'm sometimes thin-skinned and over-sensitive, so I sought out others' opinions on our day in the halls of Congress, and found they too felt disgruntled and shabbily treated. "I guess it's the times we live in," one lady said sadly.

The last day arrived and I hadn't yet had a chance to see the real Constitution. The lines at the National Archives where it was on display had been long, so on that last day I left my group to arrive when the building opened. Public buildings are open at 10 a.m., but I found on this day the building was closed to the public until noon because there was to be a symbolic swearing-in of 60 or so immigrants on the steps of the Archives.

But I'm already a citizen, my mind screamed, and I want to see MY Constitution now!

My plane was to leave shortly after noon, so I never got to see that all-important piece of parchment. It would be another six years before I ever laid eyes on that cherished document when we were on a family vacation to the nation's capitol.

I suppose the final thing to stick in my throat came during a long wait in a hot and humid airport with masses of people teeming around. We were crowded in a small area, standing patiently in line awaiting boarding of our flight. It seemed like we'd been there an awful long time. There were several older ladies in our group who were growing very tired, but everyone was being pretty decent about the whole thing, when an announcement was made that our group's boarding would be delayed because a party of 25 would be boarding ahead of the rest of us. We wondered who the lucky people would be avoiding the long lines, heat and congestion. An ID badge-wearing honcho from the State Department went sailing past security and past our group with a bunch of trade delegates from Japan. "Hey, wait your turn, dammit!" I wanted to yell. (Based on our experiences from the rest of the week, such remarks would probably have landed me in Leavenworth.)

Our wonderful, beloved Constitution, now more than 200 years old, many parts of which I memorized as a kid in a country school in Missouri, uses a phrase in the Preamble "....and secure the Blessings of Liberty." When our founding fathers used those words I'm sure it wasn't to make a flag-waving American feeling like a bomb-carrying creep.

I didn't much care for the idea of being treated like a terrorist, thank you very much!

And it still makes me mad to think about it.

Roadside Eden Destroyed

When we have visitors, which is not uncommon, they always remark on the beauty of the stretch of gravel road leading to our home.

Indeed, when Bob and I pull onto our road after a long day at work, aggravations and fatigue recede as we travel past trees, wildflowers, grasses and vines. While not so lush as country roads and lanes of bygone days when treetops touched overhead forming green tunnels through which to drive, it nevertheless has provided a soothing, soul-satisfying sight as we approach our home.

On the roadside and walking down into the moderately deep and wide ditch which has teemed with wildlife, I have taught my sons and daughters the identity of the wildflowers and other plants. When they were too young to take on long rambles into the timber, they learned near the side of the road the names of a large variety of song birds which nest in the elm, mulberry, cherry and cedar trees.

Together, my children and I have picked the blackberries, raspberries and wild plums which flourished. Elderberries grew rampant - their cream-colored flowers are very sweet smelling. In the springtime on our walks down the road, the scents which have greeted us have been the sweetest in the world: wild violets, Sweet William, wild plum blossoms and even the dainty blooms of gooseberry bushes.

Blended with the loamy smell of the small stream at the bottom of the hill - it is too modest to be called a creek, but too pretty to call a branch - the scent has created a "nose memory" for each of us, a memory involving scent when to smell it again immediately brings back thoughts of late afternoon walks down a dusty gravel road.

We've discouraged poison-sprayers, so it hasn't acquired the half-dead, fried and eroded appearance of many places which have been sprayed with herbicides. Following a time several years ago when my single hive of bees died, my tomato plants wilted and the strawberry bed also died out - all caused by county roadside spraying - the word went out: don't spray on our road.

So the roadside vegetation flourished and became quite beautiful. Birds seldom seen, such as brown thrushes, red-headed woodpeckers, goldfinches, and the rare Baltimore oriole returned and nested. Quail were even seen occasionally.

Our roadside Eden was killed last week. Violated, uprooted, torn apart, broken and scattered, it will never again be the same place. In a short time, a Warren County ecosystem was virtually destroyed by the thoughtless and capricious actions of the county road department.

Now instead of visitors marveling at the beauty of the countryside, they exclaim, "My God, what happened to your road?!"

Bethany drove home and pulled in the driveway and was crying, "Who did that to our road?" Jenny, who is at the University of Iowa where she is majoring in the environment and botany, learned of what happened to our road, and began crying. Not only does she have memories of growing up alongside a remnant of what used be a small patch of what prairies must have looked like years ago, it was also a living laboratory for her to study as she's memorized the Latin names of cone flowers, jack-in-the-pulpit, goldenseal, spiderwort, bloodroot, black-eyed Susans, violets, wild asters and little bluestem, to name a few. Our grown sons are more angry than teary-eyed.

Bob, who rarely exhibits anger, exploded. "Shouldn't property owners or nearby residents have been notified or consulted? Why was this done when we can't even get the shoulders of the road mowed?

So our small neighborhood community is left to wonder why our pretty road has been mutilated. Because not only were the plants sprayed and killed, but some sort of earth mover was brought in, uprooting trees and snapping off others, leaving the whole mess looking like something a Third World country would do to a rain forest.

Brown, dying vegetation, huge dirt-covered rootballs of trees laying over and exposed, the sod and grasses scraped from the bottom of the ditch and its slopes, which have already begun to wash and erode carrying God only knows what poisons with it into the little stream below; all caused by the ditch patrol, culvert cops who sneaked in when our backs were turned and created this insult, this massacre, this environmental stick-in-the-eye, and then left.

Incidentally, following a one-inch gully washer a couple of days later, large hunks of the road's shoulder are caving off where a blade bit into the roadbed, erosion is carving numerous grooves into the road surface, and gravel is being carried down into the bare, muddy ditch.

Everyone has memories of a special place in their childhood. Mine is Blackbird Creek near where I was raised in Missouri. It's in danger now of being polluted by giant hog farms with leaking sewer lagoons. Bob remembers woodlands and wonderful boyhood haunts from his kidhood near Beaverdale in Des Moines. Those places are long gone and are now filled with subdivisions and strip malls.

I always thought as long as we lived here on the farm I could keep one of my kids' special places intact for them. Unaware that anyone or anything could just come in and destroy wild things for no good reason, I apparently have not been a very good steward of the beautiful wild place which has meant so much to all of us.

It will take years to grow back and will never-ever be the same place.

Gambling Fever

Voters in several Iowa counties have gone to the polls to vote on whether gambling should be increased, slot machines legalized, basically everything short of legalized prostitution (and can that be far behind?) is being voted on. Indeed, voters in two river towns a few years ago voted overwhelmingly in favor of allowing no-limits casino gambling on riverboats.

I prepared a bunch of materials to refer to in my case opposing increased gambling in our fair state. In fact, I would go so far as to rescind, do away with and ban all gambling in the state. Oh, not for any noble-sounding, moral reasons; it's mostly instinct and common sense that has prompted my opposition. It may be great for the few who stand to make huge profits on others' folly and losses, but not for the thousands who patronize gambling establishments.

Plotting my column layout, I had articles from business magazines, newspapers, U.S. News and World Report and even Travel and Holiday magazine, which I was going to use in my argument on why our state should not attempt to become the new Las Vegas. All of the publications I'd gathered have carried articles on the subject and why gambling is not a good investment; how it has negative and long-lasting effects on people, communities, and main street businesses.

Travel and Holiday cited the sad example of the old Colorado mining town of Central City, which has always been a popular tourist attraction. In fact, we visited the place ourselves a few years ago and were charmed by its rustic unchanged appearance of another age.

Three or four years ago, however, the town's aging water system collapsed and it was in need of a lot of money to replace it, and quickly. Legalized gambling was introduced with the thought that proceeds would easily and painlessly pay for a new municipal water system.

The casinos were soon purchased by outside interests who didn't much care about the town, its residents, the heritage of the old mining community, or its water problems, and the place reportedly has declined considerably.

But the fact of the matter is, a column quoting other sources and using lots of facts and figures from economists, counselors, recovering gambling addicts and families whose lives have been destroyed by gambling - that type of column might be terribly dry, grim and unappealing.

So I decided to set aside my magazines and informative news articles and do what comes naturally: share my feelings in plain talk.

The thing about this gambling issue is there just seems to be something tainted and fishy about it. Many people feel as I do, and suspect that probably at least half the legislators in the General Assembly have been bought and paid for by gambling interests, ethics be damned. One legislator raises racing greyhounds, but "only as a hobby," while another has purchased riverfront property adjacent to the future location of a casino boat, but it's just a coincidence.

The gambling commission, as I understand its mission, is supposed to regulate or oversee gambling interests already in place as well as those that are proposed. The commission has been filled not by impartial business people or university economics specialists, but mostly by gambling proponents. Some fair-mindedness and objectivity we're apt to find there, I'm sure.

When gambling was first introduced into the state in the form of the Lottery, I ho-hummed. How bad could it be, I wondered, and compared it to being sort of like those little scratch-off prize things you get in a box of Post Toasties or in a Publishers Clearing House Sweepstakes offer. Besides, wasn't it going to help our schools? That's what we were told, I remember it well.

But instead of providing badly needed funding for education, I found that money from the Lottery was used as bribes - business incentives in biz-talk - by the state's development commission to bring industry into the state; industry that might stay around just long enough to use the funds and for people to feel secure in their jobs, then it would pull out or go under. Lottery funds also contributed to such things as building new NFO headquarters in Ames. A priority item, surely.

In the meantime, our schools are scrambling to find extra money, and are having to cut corners to meet budgets because they're not getting a whole lot from state coffers.

Yes, the Lottery came along, and I was indifferent, then Lotto. Somewhere along the line horse racing slipped in, both live and simulcast. Dog racing was here, but I never paid much attention to it. Who could get excited or interested in watching skinny, underfed hounds race after a plastic rabbit?

Then the riverboats entered the picture. They were to be a new attraction in the state, kind of like the Amanas or the Grotto or the Iowa State Fair. And there was a limit on how much you could lose, after all, and the riverboats looked so pretty and romantic. A throwback to another age. And the Indians had their casinos, but I never understood that. Are they sovereign or something, and don't have regulations to speak of like others, and how did they come to be so wrapped up with gambling?

So I have questioned and equivocated while the governor, the Legislature and the gambling interests performed their public mating ritual.

Then one day I was at the grocery store standing behind a woman wearing a fancy brand new black satin jacket from one of the river gambling boats.

She must have had a good weekend, I thought, and had won some money if she wanted a souvenir jacket costing more than $100. And then I watched as she paid for her soft drinks and Ragu Spaghetti Sauce with Food Stamps.

Gambling and Food Stamps do not go together. But they will and worse, if gambling is increased in this state.

Our Legislature, our state government, seems to have sold us out and has been bought off. The governor has no spine and has been back and forth as much on gambling as Bill Clinton has been on foreign policy and government clerical workers. So I really have no faith in our elected representatives guarding the best interests of the state. They care for their political fortunes and that's about it, as far as I can determine.

I think of the statistics I've read, of the increases in crime by 50 percent or more in the counties near the rivers where the casinos are located; of the huge jump in personal bankruptcies; of suicides, wrecked families, or the stories such as people leaving their small children untended or locked in cars while they gamble for hours. And this is not occurring in Las Vegas, Atlantic City or Louisiana. No, it's right here in the Midwest, in the Heartland.

There is a gambling hotline in Iowa the state is compelled to operate and its number is 1 (800) BETS OFF. The service is to help compulsive gamblers break out of their gambling habits - sometimes to keep them from blowing their brains out. Or phone counselors direct desperate callers to others for help, people who can try to help straighten out ruined marriages, jobs and bank accounts or to break the cycle of gambling. In a cruel irony, the hotline is funded by gambling revenues.

If gambling continues to grow as it has in Iowa, our state will continue a slow slide into a moral sewer.

All 'Hail' Breaking Loose

In a recent column I wrote about planting garden. I ended it with the words: "....Nothing to do now, but wait for rain and then watch it grow."

Well, that wasn't exactly how it happened as things turned out. Oh, I watched it grow after the rains came. And then the rains left, never to return, or so it seemed.

Then, lo, the rains appeared again. My garden became verdant and lush. And during early mornings as I bent over and picked strawberries, I would slowly straighten up, ease the cricks from my back and admire the nearby garden.

The peas were loaded with blossoms, the beans in their crooked rows were blooming and promised a bumper crop. My prize sweet corn was waist high, the early variety was already tasseled out, and the rest was as pretty a picture as I'd seen. And vine crops, the melons, squash, cucumbers and pumpkins were spreading and blossoming. And yes, I told the kids, I'd make plenty of dill pickles this year and they could eat as many as they wanted. And yes, I'd planted all kinds of melons from the little bitty watermelons they could go out and pick and scoop into like grapefruit, to great big ones that'd have to wait until late summer to ripen.

The tomatoes, ah, those tomatoes - more than a hundred plants of several varieties from the no-acid for Bob's wimpy palate to the huge, juicy Big Boy tomatoes - I'd can hundreds of quarts and have plenty for fresh use and to give away to friends and family.

Yessir, I was proud of my garden. I pulled weeds and hoed and rototilled and bug-dusted. I even "ridge-tilled" like the big boys, the farmers, do by pulling up dirt from between rows and banking it around onions and beans. It would protect them from sun-baking, smother weeds and preserve moisture.

It was a beautiful garden, a luscious garden, bringing pride and joy to my heart. And as any farmer can tell you, it's feelings like that which bring trouble, and court disaster and heartbreak.

It came from the northwest late one Sunday afternoon following thunderstorm and tornado warnings for western counties. We followed the bulletins on TV and watched as the storm approached southern Warren County.

Bob and the boys moved cars into available space in nearby buildings. I got out the oil lamps, checking the oil and wicks. I filled pans with water in case of power outage. At least we'd have light and drinking water. The girls kept watch for weather updates on the TV screen and got out their sleeping bags, their favorite dolls and reading books ready to take to the basement. I moved lawn chairs and a barbecue grill from the front porch to prevent them from being blown through the picture windows into the living room.

We had been through this drill before as we continued to shut storm windows and pulled down window shades in case the windows would be blown in and shattered - the blinds would help keep the broken glass from scattering so much and from imbedding in walls. I even unbent and let the long-haired, cowardly dogs in the house, shedding hair and possibly (shudder) ticks.

We waited. And it struck.

First the rain came down in torrents, then the wind came with the rain driving it in a horizontal path just like the tropical hurricanes that hit the coasts of Texas and Florida. And then that dreaded sound - hail. Bouncing little balls of ice, blown like buckshot from a 12 gauge, shredding everything it hit, tree bark, leaves, flowers, ferns, tomatoes, corn, vines.

The little girls - traumatized by a 1980 storm that had sent softball-sized hail breaking our windows, house siding, and ripping off shingles; totaling out the cars, killing trees and pets - were whimpering. The boys were strangely quiet, and soon the kids were sent to the basement. Bob was pacing and going from window to window, and I was shaking and trying not to show how worried I was. After all, I'm the one who claims to enjoy a good storm.

We listened for the ominous sound of the classic tornado roar that would send Bob and me to the basement, only to hear the repeated sound of pelting hail, wind, rain and tree branches as they hit the house. "Oops, well there goes one tree down from the windbreak," I announced, "And the driveway is blocked because of big limbs from the elm tree."

Ages later, the storm blew on past us. We waited out the lightning and rain squalls until finally that too ceased. We could go out and inspect the damage.

"Uh, Linda, why don't we just wait to go out to the garden -it'll look better in the morning," Bob suggested. But I wanted to see if the hail and wind and rain had done its worse.

It had.

Shredded, broken off, laid over in the mud, bruised, pitted, scarred, erased, my beautiful garden was gone. The dirt had even been blown off the potatoes and they could be picked off the ground.

Every day I've checked the garden to see if it was pulling out of it as old-timers have assured me it would. I'm still waiting; and replanting. But regaining my sense of humor about it now that the tears have dried.

"God did this," a friend told me, "to remind us that He's around and still in control of things."

"Well, I never doubted that," I said, "And if He wants to remind us, frankly, I'd prefer He stick with rainbows!"

Bethany: A good hay-hand.

Making Hay While The Sun Shines

Once or twice a year, considering my family lives in the country, we do something farm-related.

And it's that time of year again, the dog days of August, when the cry of locusts fills the air and a sultry haze hangs on the horizon. The days are hot and humid, and it's perfect growing weather for corn and soybeans and grasshoppers.

It's also the time of year for putting things by, to use a phrase from the old folks. And along with green beans and pickles, another thing put by is something to feed the livestock when winter snows fly and the ground is frozen hard. It's haying time in Warren County and our annual reintroduction to farm work.

I love the smell of fresh-cut alfalfa and clover - there are few smells as sweet. And with the long, sunny, dry days, it has been perfect haying weather.

Our farm is what is more commonly known as an acreage. If we were wealthy or had more class, our 30 acres would be called an estate, but I prefer to call it a farm. Considering I was raised on a working farm of 19 acres in Missouri consisting of two hills and a slough, which supported my mom, my brother and me, 30 acres could rightly be called a farm.

And to help pay property taxes, thereby keeping Warren County tax coffers comfortable, we raise hay on a portion of our 30 acres, very good hay, I might add. The first cutting of hay - we usually have three - was baled in very large bales. Those are easy to handle, mostly because the work is done by someone else. Our neighbor cuts and conditions the hay, Bob rakes it and another neighbor comes in and custom bales it. Bob moves it from the hayfield to a place on the edge of the field, and everyone is happy, particularly me, since I haven't had to get out and work with it.

The hayfield received its second cutting last week. The hay was baled in small handling-size bales, and I found myself recruited for some of the hottest, hardest, dirtiest work I can think of: picking up and stacking hay in mid-August. And, of course, haying is always done on one of the hottest days of the year.

It all began for me when I decided to show Bob I could still throw hay - I was going to walk a couple hundred feet, pick up a dozen or so bales, and then retreat to the house. There were others in the hayfield. Our neighbor was baling, Bob was driving a tractor with a hay wagon, and our neighbor's teen-aged farm hand, Tommy, was on deck. Bethany, seeing everyone out in the field, also showed up to help.

Somehow or other, I never did get to leave the hayfield to everyone else and return to the house.

The hay wagon was half full when it was determined I could drive the tractor. I'm not real comfortable with tractors, even the midsize old Ford we have. The only other time I'd driven it, it was pulling a wagon, and I'd made a turn that was apparently too sharp. The corner of the hay wagon met the wheel of the tractor in a decidedly not-supposed-to-happen way. Since that time and the tense, "never-mind-I'll-take-care-of-it-myself" injured tone Bob used with me, I've refused to have anything to do with a tractor. Until last week. As it turned out, I did a pretty fair job of driving. Oh, there were the awkward times when I let out the clutch too quickly, the tractor jerked forward and Bob and Tommy, came close to going over the back of the wagon, or had to grab hold of something. But all in all I acquitted myself quite well. I allowed at least an acre in which to make a turn and kept my eye on the tractor tire's proximity to the wagon. Furthermore, I never once killed the engine.

Bethany, too, was performing admirably. I was concerned about the sun burning her fair skin, but she had other worries besides skin. She had been cultivating her fingernails for several weeks, and they had grown remarkably and looked quite good. They are now broken off and ragged. Her arms are also scratched up from hay and she has tried to be stoic about it even while moaning, "My senior pictures are being taken next week, and I have no fingernails left, and my arms look like a leper's!"

I've tried to console her by telling her that is what retouching is all about.

Picking up hay in the field is not such a bad job. There is usually a nice breeze blowing, and swallows swoop down to catch bugs. Our dogs are off in the distance chasing rabbits or digging for something.

The really awful part of haying, in my view, is putting it in the barn. Barns are by definition protected from the weather. And that means they're usually airless and hot inside. Mix that with the hayseeds and dust filling the air, and the gut-crunching labor of hauling bales from the wagon, carrying them inside and hoisting them up to be stacked - I can get a bale only about six feet off the ground - and there is no more rigorous work a woman can do outside of the labor room, unless it's raising teenagers.

The day passed and we were later joined by our son and a buddy of his - a city boy who thought it might be fun to say he'd baled hay - and I was finally able to return to the house and fix food.

At the end of a session in the hayfield, one of the most satisfying feelings is taking a shower, washing off the sweat and prickly hayseeds and dirt. The next most satisfying feeling is sitting outdoors catching a cool evening breeze while watching lightning flash on the horizon. It could be merely heat lightning or a thunderstorm approaching.

But let it rain. Our hay is off the ground and under cover.

Until the next cutting.

Lincoln Township's Hog Dilemma

(April 1994) There is a new industry in north central Missouri among the beautiful hills where I was born and raised. It has been the cause of mixed feelings and sometimes ill will between friends and neighbors.

It's the hog-raising business, corporate-style. Not just a confinement system or a large hog lot, but hundreds and hundreds of acres given over to nothing except raising hogs. Corporate hog mega-production has pretty much taken over the surrounding counties, now it's Putnam County's turn.

Families in the west end of Putnam County fought for ages a large animal production system being placed in their neighborhoods, and I can't say I blame them.

Now it's the northeastern part of the county that's in turmoil over the threat of a large hog-raising facility being placed in its midst. But to me, this latest issue has become much more personal. This time it's taking place in my old neck of the woods, practically in the back yard of my old home, the place I was raised and knew better and loved better than any other place in the world - still do, if the truth were known.

The arguments of the hometown folks take two paths. The landowners who want the hog industry to come in are either selling their land to the corporate hog outfit or plan to. They apparently are being offered very good money for their places, much more than they would normally have expected. They're anxious to sell, eager, in fact. There is also the promise of jobs and a brighter economy for the county.

Then there are the landowners who don't want to sell their places, have no plans to, and that being the case, certainly don't want thousands and thousands of hogs as neighbors. I guess my sympathy would fall into the latter group.

In the first place, hogs are perhaps the smelliest animals on God's earth, not just stinking, but dangerous foul odors come from hog production facilities. And the hog smell and waste taints everything; it'll kill weeds and trees and grass; run-off will pollute streams, foul them and kill fish, and it doesn't do a bit of good to humans either.

When I was on the Warren County Board of Review, a property tax-appeal entity here in Iowa, several appeals on property tax assessments were filed involving vacant and unused hog-raising facilities. I remember once walking through a pig nursery where the concrete floor had disintegrated to the point it was like pea gravel, caused by the destructive, potent waste of pigs.

Another building, a steel building, contained empty pens and portable gates. The surface of everything in that building was corroded and thickly coated with rust. If the building was 10 years old, I'd be surprised, but when I looked at it, it was a weathertight, closed-up, empty, rotting-with-rust-from-the-inside building that had formerly held hogs. Just a peek was all we were allowed inside the building. It was unsafe to do otherwise since the air was too toxic to breathe. But we saw enough.

And the corrosion-causing action had to be from odor or fumes, not the actual animal waste because the under-surface of the steel roof was solidly coated with rust, too. It was spooky to look at. If it does that to steel, I wonder what it does to human tissue like lungs? Scary to think about.

Slurry pits built to hold waste from hogs, which hadn't been used for years, were still considered dangerous and toxic, and they were mostly just muck, or dried-on-the-surface muck.

That much I've seen of hog-raising facilities.

For a few years there was a comparatively small-sized hog-raising facility near our home. When the wind was in the right direction the smell of the animal waste was overpowering. On an airless, humid July day, the stench enveloped everything. The first time I caught a whiff of it I searched the house high and low, and cleaned out every closet and corner looking for where a cat might have done its dirty deed. It's THAT bad. No, it's even worse, hard as that is to believe. Laundry that was hanging on the clothesline had even absorbed the odor and had to be rewashed.

Our son once worked on the farm of a neighbor who raised hogs in confinement. I ended up burning my son's work clothes and his work boots. The smell couldn't be washed from them, even using bleach. It's THAT bad.

The automated feeding systems for hogs have to be switched on regularly, too. The equipment squeaks, clangs, screeches and whines, making quite a lot of grating, nerve-wracking noise, and who has ever known a pig to eat without squealing and banging around?

I won't try to describe the waste lagoons and slurry pits where the ungodly-smelling hog waste is carried. Suffice it to say that when I've read of an unfortunate who has accidentally slipped and fallen into one, I think there must be no more horrible way to die, because that's that happens, you die around that stuff.

No, the mass raising of hogs does not belong where people are trying to live and raise families.

Several years ago, a strip mining operation moved into my home county and bought up many of the farms and the land in the eastern part of the county, not so awful far from the proposed piggery. They tore down homes and farm buildings, gutted the land, stripped it of generations-old oaks and hickories, leveled the hills and created new ones with slag, and even filled in, rerouted and tried to kill a creek, unsuccessfully I'm happy to report. And when it was all over, the mine closed down and left town.

The folks down home - fine, hard-working people - are still suffering the effects of 15 years ago.

My roots go deep enough and my love for the people and the land where I grew up remains strong enough, I still call the place home. I think unless the long-lasting, far-reaching effects of turning much of the county into one huge hog lot and factory are carefully considered, the place will be as poorly served by the hog industry as by the coal industry.

**** *******

(A year passed after I wrote the preceding column and I once again wrote about the continuing controversy of corporate hog factories being built near my hometown. It had become much more than a proposal, however, it was a reality. The unneighborly and environmental blight of the hog factories was also spreading to Iowa and other states in the farm belt.)

March 1995 - These farms raise thousands of hogs at one time in closed confinement systems with huge sewage lagoons to take care of hog manure, or waste as it's called in polite society. The sewage lagoons are toxic and poisonous for humans, livestock, plants or any living thing to exist beside.

While waste can be claimed to be controlled, at least as to its location, the odor of hogs cannot. They smell, they stink and the ammonia-filled odor is overpowering and offensive at best, intolerable and toxic at worst.

For the past few years, the hog corporation, Premium Standard Farms, having already purchased a good-sized portion of the northern tier of counties in north central, Missouri, turned its attention further east to Putnam County, and to Lincoln Township. Lincoln Township is the place I was raised, and where I went to school; it's the township my grandmother's people settled in the 1880s, and where she and her brothers and sisters were raised. My great-grandfather farmed and operated a coal mine in Lincoln Township. A young man came to mine coal for him in 1940, boarded with my great-grandparents, met their granddaughter, and later married her. The young couple were my parents.

My brother and I were raised on a farm across the field, or about 100 yards from my great-grandfather's place. We hunted and fished, gathered blackberries and hickory nuts, and traipsed the old roads, the hills and streams of Lincoln Township when we were kids. We rode over its roads and bridges on our school bus route, and knew every inch of it when driver's licenses made us more mobile. In short, other than the place I've lived and raised my children in Warren County, Lincoln township is quite possibly the most important place on earth for me.

But much of it was purchased by the mega-hog corporation which set up its enterprise within throwing distance - just across a gravel lane - from my old home.

Some of the folks in Lincoln Township, many of them of retirement age, or even well past it, were eager to accept generous payments from PSF for their land. The rest of the people living around the proposed hog operation, after vocally objecting to it, did the unthinkable for those live-and-let-live folks of Lincoln Township: They sought legal help and then passed a zoning ordinance which would effectively have limited what could and could not be carried out in the township, mega-hog production being one of those things which was restricted. The faceless hog corporation, nevertheless, continued building more facilities. A court injunction was filed to keep the operation from starting up until environmental studies could be carried out. Regardless of that, the hog production began anyway.

Then the protesting citizens of Lincoln Township - all 146 of them -

had one last indignity visited upon them when a $7.9 million lawsuit was filed against them by Premium Standard Farms.

Many of those 146 people are well known to me. Growing up with many of them, I attended a one-room country school and later, high school with several of them. I have relatives, distant kin and shirttail cousins fighting PSF. In a sometimes awkward-feeling contrast, I also have friends and close relatives working FOR the hog company.

Opponents of the hog corporation formed an organization, "Family Farms for the Future," to combat the company, The members of the organization are neighbors and those who have had their lives, homes, livelihoods and quality of life destroyed or unalterably changed by the presence of an unwanted and uninvited neighbor, the hog-raising corporation.

Next weekend, the folks in Lincoln Township will be joined by a new ally: Willie Nelson and his Farm Aid troops will be appearing on behalf of Family Farms for the Future. Other farm organizations like PrairieFire and the Missouri Rural Crisis Center are in on the movement, too. The concert will be held eight miles northeast of Unionville, near the Lincoln Township voting precinct, the same small frame building where as a kid I spent several seemingly endless afternoons when my mother had election day duty.

Those of us with roots deeply laid down in Putnam County are having to watch from a distance and from the sidelines while this plays itself out, hoping that the land we knew and loved so well will remain unchanged. Just the other day I had a call from a friend in California. She'd lived just down the road from us when we were growing up, and our mothers belonged to the same extension club. She'd read about the hog farm controversy and the Willie Nelson concert in her local newspaper, and was concerned for old friends and the community she grew up in. A mother and grandmother now, and a resident of California for more than 30 years, she nevertheless still considers Lincoln Township her home.

A week after the announcement of the Farm Aid Rally I was left to make a decision: Would I or would I not travel to Missouri to join in support of friends and former neighbors in their dispute to keep the large corporation from beginning the production of tens of thousands of hogs, disrupting the lives and perhaps destroying the livelihoods of those living within smelling distance of it.

I really didn't have the time to kill a day traveling to Missouri to God-only-knows what type of situation. What might I find myself in the middle of? Hostility? Indifference? A cross between a hoe-down and a Baptist revival? Something on the order of a holy war?

After all, Willie Nelson was scheduled to appear at the Farm Aid rally for the beleaguered folks in Lincoln Township where the corporate pig-people had bought up hundreds and hundreds of acres. But was it really worth going south?

And then I got to thinking. There are so many things about which I feel strongly that I really don't have the guts to do anything about, except perhaps write about them. Like abortion, for instance. I would probably not consider laying in the middle of the street in front of a Planned Parenthood clinic, waiting for the law to come in, cuff me and drag or carry me off to throw me in the back of a paddy wagon. Not for me the cold floor of the local lock-up. I feel strongly about the pro-life cause, but jail and discomfort? I'm a weak and spineless being.

But hadn't I written passionately about the cause of the Lincoln Township farmers near my hometown in Missouri?

My brother, Mike, told me he heard reports on the sad situation of the hog farms trying to muscle out family farmers; he had heard interviews with our old friends and neighbors on National Public Radio. "It about blows my mind," he said, "hearing names on NPR I hadn't thought of in years."

And God knows my family has often heard me give vent to my feelings about Premium Standard Farms, the huge corporation that is buying its way into Putnam County, and into the state capital at Jefferson City through lobbying, and has probably already pocketed its share of members of the U.S. Congress.

What kind of example would I be showing my kids if I just sat back and let others join in a fight that's affecting thousands of people, not just in Missouri, but in other states - including Iowa - where those very large, faceless and impersonal transnational corporations move in and take over, contributing little to their neighbors but trouble, pollution and heartache. In fact, the Iowa Legislature is debating the issue now.

About an hour before the concert was scheduled to begin, I'd made up my mind and shouted for my teen-aged daughters, "Grab your coats, girls, we're heading for Missouri! Ol' Willie is waiting for us!" And over the miles we sped on the brisk and breezy spring day.

In my hometown things were curiously silent. This was something puzzling I'd come across on another visit I'd made down home. Usually very vocal and outspoken about most things, people were not talking at all about the upcoming concert, the hog corporation, the Lincoln Township farm families, or the multi-million dollar lawsuit filed against the farmers by the corporation. Was it indifference or something else?

But I shrugged off my concern figuring the people will be very vocal come summertime and a hot, humid day when the air for miles around is filled with the stench of thousands of hogs, and it eddies down to the low spots of the country club, and rises up to swirl around the courthouse. Or when respiratory diseases and breathing disorders begin to increase.

As we drove to the Farm Aid rally, passing the houses and farms of my old neighborhood I was so familiar with, I noticed a large United States flag flying in front of the property of an old neighbor. In front of it was a sign for all who passed by to see, "Arnaman Farms. Since 1911!"

The sign also welcomed Willie Nelson to Putnam County and Lincoln Township. At every farm on the road that runs around the perimeter of the hog operation, large U.S. flags were flying at farm homes.

We rounded a curve, and I saw the people standing and listening to country music and to guest speakers in this growing movement to save family farms.

During that afternoon I ran into people I hadn't seen in years and years as we exchanged greetings and hugs; these were former neighbors, people I went to school with, and their now-grown kids who have followed tradition farming as their parents and grandparents did before them. Their scorn and resentment of the powerful hog corporation was apparent. Their research and knowledge of the subject of hogs raised in large corporate installations, of ecology and the environment, and the politics and economics of the whole thing were wide-ranging and impressive.

There were hundreds of people from across the nation at the Lincoln Township Rally. Black farmers from Georgia and North Carolina who live in the shadow of large hog factories related stories of lives and environment ruined by corporate hog farms. The leader of the 32-tribe Indian nation of Oklahoma, the 132nd generation of his family to farm, he said, spoke of the woes that Oklahoma farm families are having with corporate farms. All the farm states of the Midwest were represented, including many from Iowa, who are experiencing their own grief with big hog farms, notably DeCoster Farms. Canada even sent a letter of support.

During one music session, I watched as a group of J. Crew-dressed kids were grooving to the country music. Probably college kids from the state university in Kirksville out to kill an afternoon, I thought. Dressed politically correct right down to Birkenstocks, one girl was trying to do some sort of dance-shuffle on squishy mud that had been topped by layers of straw. "Where does she think she is?" 17-year-old Bethany said in disgust, "At a country Woodstock?"

The afternoon was peaceful, even though every uniformed cop in five counties, including the Missouri Highway Patrol, must have been on hand.

Security for the rally was provided by Harley bikers, honest-to-God. Members of ABATE, a biker's organization were on hand to see that nothing went amiss, and that organizers of the event were not worn out by chatty, schmoozing types. With bandanas tied around their heads, bearded and wearing leather jackets and pants, and many wearing earrings, they provided a strange yet comfortable contrast to the farm families wearing Wranglers, flannel shirts, seed corn caps and hooded sweatshirts.

And yes, Willie Nelson did appear during the last half hour with no fanfare, no introduction, just the clout and attention that his name on a farm cause will attract.

I just hope that in the case of the Lincoln Township folks and other despairing farm families, it does some good.

As my daughters and I headed home for Iowa, we saw one of the most striking things we'd witnessed during the day when we passed a farm a couple of miles from the rally site. It was a U.S. flag accompanied by a large white painted sign in front of the home of a farm lady, a friend of our family, the mother of kids I went to school with, and now a widow staying on at the farm where she grew up and where she and her late husband raised their family.

From her back yard you can see the rooftops of countless hog facilities of the encroaching hog farm. A creek that once freely flowed across her property is now no more than a trickle, having been dammed up by Premium Standard.

Hers was one of the voices my brother heard on the NPR broadcast. She stays on her farm despite all the disturbances, though, this friendly, sweet-natured, white-haired lady. Some of her kids came in from distant places to be by their mother's side for the rally.

The sign they placed in front of the homeplace by the side of the road told the story of the day:

God Bless America! God Bless Family Farms!

Manners

I saw a piece on the news the other day about hand-wringing in England because of the general lack of good manners these days. Few people, the item said, appear to be aware of any type of good manners or etiquette at all. Or if they are, it isn't noticeable in public.

Obviously, this problem is apparent not just for the Brits, but in other places, as well. I, too, have noticed the trend toward generally crass and slob behavior everywhere from the talkers and hackers in theaters to the way people behave in large places like shopping malls.

I can't remember a time when I was a kid I wasn't being reminded to mind my manners. And the teaching process was on-going. My Grandpa Pollock was probably the biggest influence in my lessons of learning manners and proper behavior. And because I loved him so much, and he was so sweet and patient, it was always worth the little effort it took to remember and show off good manners just to hear his words of praise, "Well, now you're being a regular little lady!" I would just glow, knowing that I was pleasing him and making him proud of me.

And there were so many things to remember, too. Like: never take the last of anything at the supper table. Always offer a grown-up your chair. Don't talk with your mouth full. At the table, always ask for something to be passed, never reach in front of anyone for something. Always remember to say "please," and "thank-you," excuse me" and "you're welcome." And don't interrupt when others are speaking.

Boys had extra things to learn. Like: remove your hat or cap when entering a room, when a lady is present, when the flag is passing, or when the National Anthem is being played. Open doors for ladies and help ladies with their chairs. Always remember, "Ladies first," when leaving a room or going out a door. And, of course, the courtesies of pleases and thank-yous.

I miss those by-gone days. Because that's what it seems they are. Days that have passed. Very seldom do I see manners displayed anymore by kids, or for that matter, by their elders.

Men and boys alike wear their darned big cowboy hats and seed corn caps into restaurants and theaters without even thinking about removing them. They hack and hawk and snort and spit on the sidewalks for the rest of us to walk in, and those that chew tobacco, ...well, it's too disgusting to even write about.

Table manners, even in restaurants, are a thing of the past. I see guys eat like field hands half-laying over the table like someone is going to steal their plates away, shoveling in the grub with both hands.

So often in restaurants I notice the transgressions of even the most elementary table manners or public behavior.

Have you ever seen women breast-feeding in public? Now, there are those who might think that is a natural thing, and therefore beautiful. I don't happen to be one of them. There are ways to breast feed an infant without making a public display of it as if to say, "These are my large, life-sustaining, milk-laden, blue-veined breasts, and I'm proud!"

No honey, you're crude! Get that child's blanket and cover yourself up while he's nursing. That's what most of the rest of us have done.

And there are no words to express my opinion of diaper-changing in public. Or for those who throw soiled disposable diapers onto roadsides or parking lots or sidewalks. Actually, I do have the words, they're just not polite.

And the bad to non-existent manners of loud, uncontrolled, squalling, screeching children who have interrupted weddings, church services and yes, even funerals; and have ruined shopping trips and meals for those who have watched their obnoxious behavior with dismay and disgust, is unequaled at any time I can recall.

Lack of politeness or consideration of others is even exhibited on the streets and highways. Because that's what I think of when, for example, I'm following a tractor pulling a large wagon load of hay - large bales stacked two across, obscuring vision and taking up a lane and a half. Fine, they have to get to where they're taking the hay, but it seems to me, out of consideration of others, the driver could pull onto the lane-wide road shoulder, or the occasional road or driveway and allow a mile of backed-up traffic to pass. But that would be for politeness' sake, and that isn't the rule anymore.

And because I was raised to at least be aware of the more basic rules of etiquette, I've tried with mixed success to instill in my own children a working knowledge of good manners.

As it was with me and my brother, grandparents have played an important role in the teaching process. Their patience and kindness and those all-important words of praise prompted more response than my more abrupt commands as I attempted to spoon-feed a tot in a high chair, while keeping milk glasses full, wiping up a glass of spilled milk and making sure nobody was sneaking food to the waiting maw of the dog under the table.

I can think of few words that make me feel prouder as a parent than to hear, "Your kids have the nicest manners." And I think to myself, "Well, I'm glad SOMEONE has seen them!" since manners around home are generally displayed when grandparents or elderly people are visiting. Only rarely are they on exhibit for parents, except when they want something. Then it becomes more a matter of good marketing than good manners.

As they've grown up I've told our kids about good manners and politeness and how they're appreciated by friends, sweethearts, in-laws and prospective employers.

People might not remember you because of your intelligence, smooth style and wit, or your fine clothes, but they WILL remember good manners and courtesy.

Sometimes I think in my secret heart of hearts they might have listened to me.

Small Adults And Answering Machines

It was one of those Monday national holidays when Bob was off work, and the girls didn't have school because of teacher in-service; Des Moines schools were also out, only because of the holiday; and I had taken the day off. We had driven in to the capitol city for a day of shopping and perhaps would tour some places of interest.

To start the day off as something a little special, we were eating breakfast out at McDonald's in one of the suburbs.

"Psst, Mom," Jenny said. I looked up at her from the front page of the paper I was scanning. "Look at the little boy over there," she said. "He's eating breakfast all alone!" I glanced over at the table across from ours, and sure enough, there was a little boy eating his pancakes all alone. The kid might have been eight, and there was no hint of poverty about him; we were in one of the more upscale suburbs, and any place the kid would have walked from was not poor. He was wearing name-brand hightops and NFL sweats.

"This might be an example, Jenny," I explained to my daughter, "Where a holiday and kids being home from school is considered a nuisance and an inconvenience by a lot of parents. That kid is probably on his own for the day, because his mom - and maybe there is a dad in the picture, too - is working. The kid's mother probably doesn't want to waste a day of sick leave or vacation when she can give the boy a five-dollar bill and there's HBO on TV."

Unfair or not, that is the way I imagined the situation, and I don't feel I was far off base as I explained it to my daughter. Still, though, I had the niggling feeling I might have been a little harsh on the unknown parent of the young boy who was eating his breakfast alone - the sight of which shocked my 18-year-old daughter.

And then I read a story in the paper, "The incredible shrinking childhood of today's children," reporting how today's young children are more or less being left to raise themselves and their siblings while their parents are off pursuing careers or a larger, grander piece of the American dream. Kids are not being allowed to be kids any longer.

There are situations, I'm aware, where single mothers have to work to support their families, and who have too much pride to take the welfare route; or whose husbands are ill or laid off and then Mom becomes the support of the family. I was raised in such a family.

And then there are couples who, even as they're planning their families, are looking into day care so they can continue their jobs or pursue their careers before their babies have begun to sleep through the night.

And I wonder why. Some say it's because women don't really want to be mothers anymore; they want children, but not the work and trouble they take to raise. They want to dress them up and play house, but want somebody else to feed them their Gerber's, wipe their runny noses and potty-train them.

But what I see are couples who want children, but as much as they want children, they want THINGS, too. They want fine clothes, a fine house filled with expensive furniture, appliances and the latest video and stereo equipment. They want at least two nice cars; they want to eat out and not just at Hardee's or Burger King. They want to take trips and dress their kids in designer jeans and $140 athletic shoes.

And once they get one thing acquired and payments arranged, they find something else, and soon they don't remember the family they yearned for. And many are too tired to do much more than kiss their kids good night after picking them up at day care.

Slowly but surely, a credit card or the "Here's $5, go buy your breakfast," has become the order of the day. There's no reading "The Cat in the Hat," or watching Sesame Street together; no teaching table manners, or having someone waiting at the door as a kid comes home from school just bursting to tell all the things which occurred during the day.

Now kids are no longer kids. They're small adults with answering machines, Post-It notes and cellular phones instead of Mom and the smell of tuna casserole at the door.

My friends and I find ourselves looking at young families today and saying, "Remember when our kids were little....?"

When our kids, many of whom are just beginning their families, were little, my friends and I, nearly without exception, stayed at home with our babies, our tots, our school kids. All of us were married and our husbands worked. Some of them farmed, some worked at factories in Des Moines, some were self-employed. My husband was in maintenance at the Post Office. Paychecks were usually turned over to wives; or at least in our household. I juggled things around and paid bills first, and then figured out what was left for groceries and spending money of which there was very little.

The kids each had one good dress outfit, a couple of second best and lots of grubbies, all of which were handed down to the next one when outgrown. They wore J.C. Penney's Plain Pocket jeans and generic athletic shoes. Garage sales were a regular shopping stop on pay week, and yes, we lived payday to payday, with no regular savings program other than Savings Bonds.

I made most of our meals from scratch, and raised a garden to feed the family. I'm not boasting. What I did was not exceptional since nearly everyone else was doing the same. We rarely ate out. There was no keeping up with anyone else, because everyone else was in the same boat, living frugally or broke. But we were home with our kids and we were generally happy.

I noticed things changing when kindergarten went to all-day. Moms began going to work to get those little extras - extras which were not really necessary, but were wants, and were soon considered essential. And those messy, troublesome little creatures called children began getting in the way. That's why schools catch hell when they close because of the weather - that leaves folks faced with a choice of finding a sitter when the school doesn't fill the need, or of leaving kids home alone or with money to buy breakfast, just like the little boy at McDonald's that concerned my daughter.

It saddens me that little kids can't be little kids any more, and that many moms today are being worn out trying to be all things to all people instead of what they set out to be: Nurturers of their young children.

photo by Bob Nandell

Stalking The Wild Morel

I was probably 11 or 12 years old the first time I ever saw a morel mushroom; only they weren't called morels, just mushrooms. And although we'd heard that people in the city actually ate mushrooms which looked like toadstools, the only mushrooms we considered fit to eat were the tasty, dipped-in-batter-and-fried morel mushroom.

The first time I saw a morel - which looks just like a cone-shaped sponge - was as it sat atop a dishpan full of cow greens picked by my uncle and aunt. Their family lived right across the field from us and ran a considerably more lax household than my mom. They and a bunch of their rollicking friends had been out on a river bottom expedition spending a fine spring afternoon fishing and picking greens and mushrooms.

{Regrettably, cow greens, a spring-time green found on creek bottoms and similar to spinach, don't grow in Iowa, or not that I've been able to find.}

From that first sight of mushrooms, not to mention the taste of them,

I've spent every spring since seeking them out for the two weeks or so the season lasts.

My brother and I always went to Blackbird Creek bottom to look for mushrooms. If we got more than enough for a "mess," which is what portions of things like mushrooms or fish are measured in rather than quarts or pounds, we would share them with others who couldn't get out; like Frank and Marie Galloway, the elderly couple who lived on the way to the creek. Marie usually had a good supply of cookies on hand, and the water from their kitchen pump tasted so nice and cold to a hot and thirsty kid on the way back home from the creek.

In high school, when to even admit to enjoying going out in the timber and creek bottoms to hunt mushrooms was not considered terribly cool, or at least to the town-kids, I went anyway. Only I took my steady boyfriend with me with my brother tagging along because Mama sent him with us. Looking back, my mother's ploys were not terribly subtle.

Later on, I introduced my city-boy husband to mushrooming, and he became an avid hunter. He won't eat them, but he loves to find them. The aggravating thing is when I think a spot is barren and impatiently move on, Bob will stand quietly in the same spot I've been and find dozens. And he never gets excited about finding them, just very calmly stoops and picks them up by the hand full. Whereas, if I find more than three in one spot, I whoop and shout, "Hot diggedy damn, I've found the mother lode!"

When my children began arriving I took them with me on mushroom-hunting trips. Sometimes they were blanket-wrapped infants; another spring they were toddlers who rode piggy-back or who had to be carried the last stretch home, as we slipped and slid down gullies and ravines or climbed over logs. Even as very cool high-schoolers, my girls would take time from their busy homework, track and social seasons to go with me. Jenny probably enjoyed getting out in the woods more than her younger sister, Bethany. Bethany's idea of a day in the wilderness and among the wild things is shopping at the mall during clearance sales.

Nevertheless, whether I'm alone, with Bob, or have one or both of the girls with me, there's enjoyment and wonder smelling the perfumes of wild flowers and growing things, or discovering the wonders of finding jack-in-the-pulpit or May apples. I've passed on the same stories and woods-lore to my kids as my mom and grandma passed on to me, as indeed generations have passed down knowledge of the outdoors from one to the other in my family.

We moved out to our farm in Warren County in April, 1970, just in time for mushroom season. I was quite pregnant at the time with our third baby. Our son, Tim, was a toddler and his brother, Mike, had just turned three. I can still remember finding my mushroom ground one warm afternoon as I carried Tim and held Mike's hand, pulling him along up a steep hill, my uphill strides bringing my leg up to bump into my large stomach on the long-hauls. It was a good time, but I thought we'd never make it home.

That was the year I received one of the nicest Mother's Day gifts when Bob took Mike on his first fishing outing. They came home in the evening fishless, but Bob carried his shirt in and it was full of mushrooms which he presented to me as if they were long-stemmed roses. To me, they were better than roses.

A mushroom hunter's ground is secret and considered just short of sacred and hallowed. The last couple of years or so, I've had trespassers on my mushroom hunting place. Nothing can get me as steamed as finding the stems of large mushrooms I know I didn't pick, the stems going to waste because someone has picked just the cone-top.

Whoever it is has large shoes, smokes Winstons and drinks Bud Light, and probably carries a walking stick because of impressions left on the ground. So, not only is the person a trespasser, but a slob-litterer as well. I notice all these things with the attention of a true mushroom fiend. And I figure this too shall pass as I place a curse on the littering intruder: I hope you run into a multiflora rose bush, and may you answer the call of nature in a patch of poison oak.

Otherwise, I'm a caring and sharing person.

The Great Outdoors? No Thanks

In a call home one day, and with absolutely no forewarning, Bob revealed alarming plans to me. "I'm off work for Veterans Day," he said, "So I thought we'd get up real early that morning, hook up the boat and drive to the lake in Missouri for a day of fishing....I knew you'd be really excited about my plans." And I thought I heard an evil chuckle in his voice.

Fishing in November. Wow. Fishing at any time. Golly-gee-whiz. But what could I say? It was his day off, and he wanted my company.

There have been other times like this. I recall once, before we began boycotting Iowa's state parks because of the extortionate user-fees, we visited Lake Ahquabi on a cloudy, damp and chilly November day for an afternoon of fishing. Bob happily fished while I huddled in a sleeping bag in the bottom of the aluminum fishing boat and read a murder mystery.

Possessing a lurid imagination, I squinted up at Bob and nodded toward a tall hilltop overlooking the lake as our anchored boat bobbed around. "See that hill?" I asked. "What if there was a nut up there looking down at us through the scope of his high-powered rifle? We'd be sitting ducks. Let's go home." This hypothetical creepy idea drew very little response from Bob except he did a very uncharacteristic thing for him when he looked up at the hill and made a naughty digital gesture at my imaginary stalker. And I ended up scaring myself and beginning to think there might really be someone on the hill peeking at us, like the movie, "Friday the 13th," only this was at Lake Ahquabi.

This thing of communing with Nature by sitting and watching for a fish that isn't there is an old story in our family. Unless I give up all pretense of being interested in fishing now that the kids are all old enough to bait their own hooks or retrieve any errant fish, I'd rather turn to a good juicy novel to read.

But usually I'd just as soon stay at home in a warm house, bake bread, sew a fine seam or read the paper. Even when called upon to share an adventure at home, I much prefer the shelter of the house instead of outside in the blustery wind and elements. For instance, on a recent Sunday, Bob was outside working on our sewer line. I knew in my heart of hearts he'd call me if for no other reason than to hold something messy, so I kept my Sunday church clothes on and didn't change into jeans. Besides, why did we have sons who eventually turn into strapping teenagers if not to help out with strenuous chores?

I've pretty much been this way all my life.

When I was a kid, there came a time of the year which brought an activity I absolutely dreaded. Even today I can feel a certain touch of frost in the air, sniff the scent of crisp fall leaves and corn husks, and my memories come back of the awful chore of picking up corn the picker missed.

Our mom would roust my brother and me from our warm beds early on a cold Saturday morning in order for us to go out in the cold weather and pick up field corn from the ground. "Gleaning" I believe it was called in biblical times. Torture it was called to a 12-year-old. And these mornings never occurred during a warm Indian summer day, but always on a cold, late fall day. This was in the days before grain dryers when corn was left to stand in the field longer to rid it of excess moisture before it was picked.

We'd arrive at the field with big, old five-gallon buckets and burlap gunny sacks and begin picking up the corn the picker had either knocked down or missed altogether. And you'd be surprised just how inefficient these handy-dandy farm implements were and how much corn they missed. I know I certainly was.

I can still remember whining all the while I was picking up corn. I wasn't usually a whiner, but picking up corn on a cold Saturday morning in a wet, sloppy cornfield when all my friends were probably home in a warm house watching cartoons on television and eating bacon and eggs and, no doubt, baking powder biscuits, too? Well, it just wasn't fair!

We would watch our scattered piles of corn grow as we traveled back and forth with heavy buckets banging against ankle bones. I would occasionally throw corn at the pile and accidentally hit my brother in the side of the head with an ear of corn. He'd return the favor, and the fight would be on with Mama yelling, "The longer you kids fool around, the longer we're going to stay here." That reminder would cause us to rededicate ourselves to making our corn piles bigger. "Aren't we about done, Mama?"

The corn we gleaned was the feed for our two milk cows, Spot and Wienie, as well as the chickens and my brother's sow. And although I loved those animals I never understood why they weren't satisfied with, in the cow's instance, pasture grass.

Years and years later in Warren County, Iowa, with children of my own, I can easily understand and sympathize with their groans when their dad announces at the Saturday breakfast table, "I think this would be a good day for us all to go out and cut wood - bundle up everybody!"

A Walking Political Error

The trend toward political correctness has become laughable when it isn't downright ridiculous. Thank God the trend appears to be reversing itself, and not a moment too soon.

A recent news report reminded me once again that politically correct speech can cloud waters and is terribly distracting. The report was about the theft of a wheelchair belonging to an eight-year-old girl. That she was disabled or handicapped goes without saying and should have been obvious because of the wheelchair.

The Channel 8 news reader, however, had to beg the question by adding to the report that the little girl was "physically challenged and visually impaired."

I am not making this up and would never joke about such a thing. But please, I need some relief from all this babbling. "Physically challenged and visually impaired?" Did the news reader mean to say the child was crippled and blind? Then why did she just not say so? Or boil it down sensitively to "handicapped" since the word "crippled" is totally incorrect, sensitively speaking. Apparently "handicapped" is an impolite word these days, also. But because of the terms used in the news report, rather than feeling immediately sorry for the little girl and her family, I was distracted and irritated by the words of the news reader.

There are so many new and correct terms to use anymore, so many sensitive things to be aware of for those of us who are walking political errors.

A lot of the terms are dreamed up in the education system to deal with truants or kids who really don't want to go to school or study or cope with things like rules, schedules or discipline.

There's a disorder called "attention deficit disorder." Exactly what does that mean? Does it mean a scatterbrain, a daydreamer, one whose mind wanders? There were students with that disorder when I was in school. They spent a lot of time writing things on the blackboard to get their attention in order when there was a deficit in that department. Today, I would imagine students such as these would get a special teacher paid for out of a pricey entitlement funds-pool. But in the 1950s, early-60s, these problems were corrected without drugs or rehabilitation or special teachers. Discipline is what it was called. It didn't do a thing to enhance their self esteem, but you know something? It must have worked because most of them snapped right out of it.

Politically correct older people are no longer senior citizens, golden-agers or the elderly; they're now known simply as "seniors" which I confuse with high school 12th-graders. I've spent quite a bit of time reading news stories which have some eye-grabbing phrase like "New benefits for seniors," because I think I'm going to read about a new scholarship or college aid program until I get to something about Medicare, usually near the end of the article.

Questions of race are minefields, and aren't doing a thing to help ease what is - and of this I can assure unaware sociologists and naive drumbeaters - the undeniable tension between the races these days.

What is the politically correct term for blacks anymore? African-Americans? People of color? I've asked this question of my friends who are, in fact, more brown than black, and they're frankly not too certain of their ancestral origins. Or what should I call an oriental? Or is it Asian? Of my Asian/oriental friends, one is of Japanese descent, born and raised in Colorado; the other's background is Taiwanese, but she's a Californian. Or my Russian son, our foreign exchange student? His father is a Tartar with a cultural heritage which is Moslem and perhaps more Arab than not; his mother springs from the more European side of Russia, and is Christian or Russian Orthodox. I dare PC police to tackle that one.

I work in a place where cultural and ethnic diversity are watchwords. I work with all kinds of people, Asians, blacks, Hispanics, men and Methodists. And I get along with all of them. Because the one secret to getting along with others, no matter how different they may be from me, is to treat them as I would anyone else. Unless, of course, they're jerks. But it's getting so you can't treat jerks as jerks anymore unless they're white jerks - and God knows there are still enough of them around - because then you're branded a racist or a bigot.

Political correctness is taking a lot of the fun out of being around ethnically and culturally diverse people. Mincing around and dancing around issues, words, phrases and the like make spontaneous conversation next to impossible. That's why I'm glad there's a move on to hoist political correctness up on the gibbet it so richly deserves.

Then quite possibly I can talk to "people" again without worrying unduly that I'm offending or stepping on toes or might be accused of being racist, bigoted or insensitive.

I've come across one politically correct term which surely takes the cake as far as I'm concerned and has been causing quite a few chuckles among my friends. It's found in the story of what I call the Manassas Whacker, the case of the Manassas, Va., wife who took a knife to her husband's nether regions. The word in the Newsweek magazine report of the case - and it is one of the most entertaining pieces of journalism I've read, although I'm still not sure if it was tongue in cheek - described the Manassas husband, the whackee, or the victim in this affair, as being "sexually challenged."

Well, if he wasn't before he certainly is now.

But sexually challenged? I'd call him lucky.

Reflection of a small world. *photo by Bob Nandell*

Saving My Corner Of The Planet

Observations of Earth Day and Earth Week and celebrations of environmentalism have passed and we can at last breathe a sigh of relief.

I'd grown weary of all the rock stars and politicians, the celebrities and grand-standers touting a subject that many of us have been wringing our hands over for years, and about which we've quietly been doing what we can.

The world we live in, and into which I brought my children, is something very dear to my heart, and I don't need to be reminded of it by a special day or a special week or a special anything.

Easter Sunday morning, practically on the very eve of the Earth Day observance, we were traveling to Missouri for a family dinner. We were driving through a neighboring county in south central Iowa, a place that not many people would think of as environmentally unsound. Except perhaps for a few like myself who remember the steep hills there which used to be covered with timber.

Now all the timber has been clear-cut; there's not a tree left standing on those steep, eroding hillsides. It's a cornfield now, or a corn-hill. There aren't even waterways in small gullies, places that will very shortly qualify for the term ravines.

What topsoil remains on the hillsides is filling in the little creek at the bottom. Only it's not a little creek anymore. It, too, was clear-cut of all the willows, scrub and brush that held its banks together. Now it's a mud-choked trough.

Across the road from these hundreds of acres of eroding hillsides is another field. Here it appears that some effort at soil conservation is being made because no-till planting is being implemented.

At least I assume that's why hundreds of acres of pasture and hay ground have been treated with an herbicide, killing all the vegetation, turning the formerly green alfalfa to a dry, dead brown.

My husband told me that he'd read where the herbicide is really a very helpful chemical, and has few residual effects.

I pointed out to him that while planting corn using herbicide and no-till equipment is seemingly quite noble, the thing that disturbed me about the ground I was looking at were the trickles of water from recent rains running off the field - I was seeing trickles as we drove by - and the trickles all came together at the foot of the slopes and formed a healthy stream that ran into a culvert under the road on which we were traveling. The stream then entered a nice winding little creek I've often remarked on to my family for its prettiness.

The little creek runs into a large lake where our family has been planning for ages to picnic and fish. But my enthusiasm for that activity is diminishing when I consider the lake water is probably laced with herbcide. And if the ag-chemical can turn a healthy alfalfa field brown, what could it do to me and my family, or to the fish in the water, or the cattle I see drinking from the creek a few hundred feet downslope from the treated and dying fields.

My mind skipped ahead to Missouri, to the hills where I grew up as a kid, where my brother, cousins and I roamed. Even my mom, as well as my grandmother and her brothers and sisters, worked and played on the same hillsides, the same fields when they were growing up.

I remember my great-grandfather, who settled the old home place, going squirrel-hunting under those large old oaks and hickories. I remember hickory-nut hunting on the way home from school, and filling lunch buckets with the nuts. Cowboys and Indians, and hide-and-go-seek were played up and down the draws and hillsides.

We played in the nearby branch, waded in it, and dammed it up with rocks and clay for a water hole to splash in on hot summer days. Arrowheads and stone ax-heads were found on the hillsides. May apples and mushrooms, Sweet William and Dutchmen's britches, bluebells and violets grew thick, and the air always smelled so sweet.

But now the generations-old oaks and hickories of the old home place have been cut down. All of them. New owners without the wisdom or common sense to be good stewards of this rough but hospitable land destroyed the trees. Or perhaps it was greed which caused the steep hillsides to be stripped of all the trees, which were then cut up and sold for firewood. Firewood. My God.

The hillsides were not only stripped of trees, but cleared of stumps and grass cover, and are slowly washing down into the little branch that brought us so much enjoyment.

While I applaud the efforts of citizens to save dolphins and whales, encourage the use of biodegradable-anything, preserve the rain forests of the Amazon and protect the ozone layer, my interest in Saving The Planet remains closer to home.

Save the trees and the fields that generations have known and loved forever. Keep for us the sweet smells of springtime in the Midwest. Don't spray and clear our roadsides, stunting and killing the trees and undergrowth that harbor birds and wildlife, destroying berries, vines and wildflowers.

These things may not fatten bank accounts or increase the Gross National Product. They do something more important.

The bring pleasure and nourish our souls.

The front porch, a summertime retreat.

Welcome To My Porch

Several years ago my husband made me an offer I couldn't refuse. It was that wonderful summer of the bicentennial year of 1976 and I was very pregnant at the time. He gave me a choice of a gift for our home. Did I, he asked, wish for an air conditioner or a front porch? It took me hardly any time at all to respond to the question. I wanted a front porch!

I had yearned for one for ages. Our home was a new split-level. It had looked so fine on a blueprint, but in reality it looked so, well, new and modern, bare, stark, characterless, unloving. In other words, it looked like thousands of tract houses in cracker box subdivisions across the country.

The addition of the front porch made the difference, sort of giving our home a personality. A porch swing was installed and the final touch was added when I planted wild cucumber vines around the porch and trained them to climb strings I'd strung up the sides of the porch. The vines, native to my home state of Missouri, had been dug up from a creek bottom on a visit to my mom.

The vines quickly grew and flourished, and soon a leafy green nook was created. Many hot afternoons were spent on that front porch as I awaited the arrival of our baby while watching our three little tow-headed boys play in the yard, or sit by me on the swing as we caught an afternoon breeze.

The tradition of a front porch has always been a part of my family. My Great-grandpa Hunt's large old house, the home place where my grandma and her brothers and sisters were born and raised, featured a big wraparound front porch on two sides of the house. The porch, surrounded by trumpet vines and bridal wreath, was the family gathering spot when I was growing up.

Countless meals were eaten on that porch, hundreds of chicken bones were furtively thrown to awaiting dogs, and millions of watermelon seeds were spit over the side. Trike races and how-high-can-we-swing were performed by my cousins and me. That is, if Great-Grandpa wasn't around. He had a glass eye and a cane, and was quite stern where kids were concerned. We didn't want to look in one or feel the other, so if Grandpa was near we'd play more quietly.

My Grandma and Grandpa Pollock had a front porch, too, in their big old farm house, only their front porch was never used. Neither was their front door, except by strangers or vacuum cleaner salesmen. No, their back porch was the place to be and it was special since it was screened in. I don't have to even think real hard to come up with a mental picture of Grandma and Grandpa sitting in their chairs on the porch in the evening or after chores; Grandpa in his bib overalls, and Grandma in her sundress and apron, as they quietly sat and read their papers. A little girl could bring her paper dolls out along with some cookies, plop down and think Great Thoughts as she shared the quiet time of early evening with the sounds of bullfrogs and crickets and the call of the whippoorwill.

When I was a kid our home had a front porch, too. We lived right across the field from my great-grandfather and my Uncle Kenneth's family, and although our front porch was of considerably more modest proportions than theirs, it was nevertheless a wonderful place. Our porch had a blue ceiling as did many porches then. Why blue became the choice of ceilings I don't know, but blue it was. Our porch was nearly ground level and there were sweetly-scented old-fashioned purple petunias around it, and hollyhocks. Hummingbirds would come and feed at the petunias and we'd sit quietly and watch them. Occasionally my brother and I would try to catch one by sneaking up with an overturned milk bucket and try to trap it. It can't be done.

Climbing up strings to protect porch-setters from late afternoon hot sunshine were the hardy wild cucumber vines, gathered in the early spring from the nearby creek bottom.

Summer afternoons would find me curled up with a book or comic on the porch, or laying down and watching clouds drift by. The front porch was also where we shelled peas, snapped beans, pitted cherries, churned cream, and cracked walnuts. It was a resting place, a visiting place and a work place.

My children are going to have their own porch memories. Over the years, our summertimes grew to be spent on the front porch. Together, our family of seven would sit there and watch rainstorms approach and hit. We enjoyed the feel of the wind and the mist of rain which occasionally blew in on us. The porch was the place where I placed the kids to snap beans or shell peas. Inevitably, it was the place the dog would have a litter of pups, or the cat would drag in her litter of kittens.

Hot summer nights would find the kids dragging blankets and pillows outside on the porch to sleep where it was cooler.

Then came the time a few years ago when we were going to put new siding on the house. What should we do about the porch, Bob asked. Over the years those trees which we'd planted when the kids were all little had grown quite large and provided shade for the entire yard and house. The porch had grown shabby-looking and between the shade trees and the porch roof little light was allowed into the house. Our living room looked like a darkened morgue. I was sick of the porch. "Let's tear it off and have a front patio instead," I suggested.

Today, we have a large stone-floored patio with a white picket fence around it; window boxes filled with petunias and impatiens, and pots of ferns and pansies flourish. We entertain on our front patio now. Our friends and neighbors know they will get a warm welcome and cold beer or iced tea as we sit and chat outdoors.

At mealtimes, when the house is too stuffy or becomes too crowded, we sit outside on the patio. At other times, Bob and I will sit outside enjoying each other's company as we catch an early evening breeze and watch the hummingbirds flit around the flowers, while a mama wren perched on a nearby limb scolds the kittens who are entertaining us by their playful antics.

On reflection, I guess the patio isn't much different than the old front porch. The only difference appears to be that it has no roof except blue skies and maple leaves.

Radio Days

Kids today have a wealth of things to keep them entertained. There are stereos, television, video games, rental movies for the videotape recorder, and if all else fails, books.

Let me take you back, though, to a few years ago when entertainment and information were provided on the radio. I am fortunate to be just old enough to remember what was to be the last of the golden years of radio.

When I was a little girl growing up in the hills of northern Missouri, we didn't have television. Oh, it was around, but only in cities or in the homes of families better off than ours.

But we had the radio. Many of the radio sets then were in large wooden cabinets taking up as much floor and wall space as big-screen televisions today.

Our radio, however, was plastic, a Philco. It was about the size of a bread box with a brown knit fabric across the front to cover the speaker. Radios had tubes then, not solid-state circuitry. Turning on a radio would not gain instant sound; first, the tubes had to warm up.

The radio in our house always sat on top of the refrigerator, a protected place from my brother and me if we decided to fight over what we wanted to listen to. Later, the radio had an honored place on a doily-topped table and sat between a potted geranium and the family Bible.

Our family listened to "Gunsmoke" and "The Lone Ranger," "Truth or Consequences," "People Are Funny," "The Great Gildersleeve," "Our Miss Brooks," Arthur Godfrey, Jack Benny, Amos and Andy, and so many others that I couldn't list them even were I to remember them.

I can still see my mom standing at the ironing board as she listened to the soaps, "Stella Dallas" is the only name I recall of those programs, and they were always sponsored by, well, soap: Ivory, Palmolive and Halo Shampoo.

As we listened to the adventures, serials, comedies, mysteries, quiz shows and variety shows, all we had to entertain us were voices and sound effects. Our imaginations came up with the scenery, the atmosphere, and peoples' appearances and costumes.

Years passed and television came on the scene. But still, except in the evenings, we listened to the radio. Our favorite stations - probably because they came in more clearly than others, now that I reflect on it, were WHO in Des Moines and KCMO in Kansas City.

Rock and roll music was born in the mid-1950s, and a few years later I began enjoying it at about the same time I started noticing boys. Baptist and Pentecostal preachers back then claimed there was probably - well, almost certainly -a connection. I began listening to rock and roll music and always tuned in to AM-940, KIOA in Des Moines. That was the only station cool people like teen-agers listened to. In the evenings, cool people such as myself, listened to rock and roll on KAAY in Little Rock or WLS in Chicago. KSO in Des Moines was another popular rock and toll station; today, of course, it is solid country music.

KOMA in Oklahoma City, or the stations in San Antonio or Nashville, which must have had strong signals to reach out to Missouri, played honky tonk, cowboy songs and the Grand Ol' Opry. Country music was not considered cool, and few teens admitted to listening to those stations.

But the mainstay of my family's listening habits was WHO in Des Moines. The dial could be moved, other music preferred, but always - even the littlest kids - knew where 1040 was, the Voice of the Middle West. "From Coast to Coast and Border to Border and Then Some." We knew the station's slogans by heart.

When I was little, I thought Des Moines in general, and WHO in particular, would be the most wonderful place to visit. In this time before things like radio signals and recorded music even entered my mind, I thought people like Patti Page, Frank Sinatra and Art Linkletter lived in Des Moines, and were actually at the WHO radio station.

We listened for the familiar voices we trusted so much like Jack Shelley, Keith Kirkpatrick or Herb Plambeck to let us know about the weather, school closings, disasters, news and the price of corn.

During the times I would stay with my grandparents, at lunch time a deep silence would descend, plates stopped rattling and forks would be suspended while my grandpa listened to the latest farm market reports at noon.

I remember how thrilled I was when my mom and her Extension club were on the Betty Baker Show on WHO - it was a woman's show featuring recipes, household hints and special guests, as I recall - and we actually heard Mama speak on the air. I can't remember exactly why she and the other club ladies had gone to Des Moines, when at the time driving up from Missouri was considered a major trip. Today, it's an afternoon shopping jaunt for many.

These days we have several radios in our house. The clock radio wakes us in the morning. The wake-up station, however, is the same I heard first thing in the morning when I was a kid, WHO, the Voice of the Middle West, as we listen to learn what has happened overnight, what the road conditions are or the weather forecast for the day.

KIOA continued to be our rock and roll icon for 30-some years with the "Good Guys" as the DJs were called, playing golden oldies; our kids grew up listening to it until they acquired their own music tastes. KIOA's Dic Youngs, aka the Youngster or Youngsie - who's been at the station for ages - and I have reached middle age together. No, I have never met the man, but I've awakened to his voice, done housework with his music and have written columns accompanied by his voice. I feel I know him.

Things have changed considerably. No longer does KIOA-AM play golden oldies - in fact it doesn't even have the same call letters; it has become a talk radio station, of all things. Now it features that old spook, G. Gordan Liddy, and an array of caustic, cynical, vulgar old poops early in the morning. If we want our rock and roll, we have to scan the FM stations for KIOA.

I think radio programming is one of those things which has not improved with age. The golden years will soon be forgotten by everyone except those of us who grew up to the sound of a radio entertaining or informing us or just keeping us company.

Cons And Scams

We recently received a letter which had big red letters at the top: "COLLECTION NOTICE - Immediate Action Requested. ALERT! Account past due." It included other threatening and intimidating language demanding the $9.97 owed the company.

And all for an expired magazine. That's right. In lieu of sending an expiration notice, the travel magazine had stooped to the ploy of sending out a "collection letter" to gain subscription renewals.

Now to the inexperienced or naive, a letter such as the one we received would definitely sound alarming. My daughter received one like it for a celebrity magazine when she was 14. The notice scared her. She didn't have the money and didn't want to ask us for it, but was afraid it would put a black mark on the credit record we have constantly reminded our kids should be kept clean and blemish-free.

So she gathered her courage and tearfully showed me the letter. Needless to say, we did not renew the subscription, but the company did receive a letter from me, suggesting creative new uses for their rag.

I could see such tactics alarming older people who have forgotten to renew a subscription or who had no intention to, and then mailing in a check because of the misleading - some would call it deceitful and dishonest - collection notice. I know it would have worried my grandmother into a nervous fit, and my mom would stew over it for days and probably make an unnecessary long-distance call to some phone subscription-hack and try to straighten things out.

Another surprise arrived in the mail containing a Wisconsin resort vacation package we had been awarded - its value was $627.90! Smelling something not quite right, I began to read it. "There are no gimmicks in this letter.....There is no obligation to purchase anything.....No obligation.....No pressure.....Honest."

It certainly sounded straight-forward enough, which is why I immediately suspected some sort of fleecing.

According to the material, everyone was eligible to accept the resort vacation prize except minors (naturally), resort employees and their families, resort property owners or those who had toured the resort in the past year.

Well, that sounded reasonable enough. Then I noticed another group of people excluded from accepting the prize: Those with a combined family gross income BELOW $35,000.

Well! We certainly don't want to be around riffraff earning less that 35-big ones, such as our grown children and many of our friends, do we? We would not be bumping into many in the newspaper business, for sure. So, in essence, this resort was for snotty, pretentious suburbanites to go so they could slap mosquitoes and drink gin and tonics.

A restricted resort with a red-line policy? No thanks.

If I want to be insulted and probably cheated, I don't have to travel to Wisconsin. Those services can be obtained closer to home.

Wood Stove Pleasures

The heating season is growing to a close, thank goodness, and many of us can begin to breathe a sigh of relief. Not only do the heating bills diminish, but we who heat with wood can begin to breathe clear air.

Clear air was not the case in the middle of the night recently as we awoke to the screech of the smoke alarm, our dog was nervously whining, and the smell of smoke was in the house. The wind had apparently changed and caused a downdraft which resulted in our stove belching out a cloud of smoke.

We didn't always have a wood-burning stove. When we built the house, we had all-electric heat. It was supposed to be the cheapest, most efficient, cleanest, safest type of heat. The cheap part changed when the Arabs embargoed oil in the early 70s. And electric heat may be efficient and it may be clean, but I never really felt warm. There was no warm air; nor a flame, or a glow that I could actually see or feel, so I was always goosebumpy.

We changed our heating source to a gas furnace later, but it didn't help much with the energy bill, and with the thermostat set at an affordable level, I was always bundled up in sweat socks and sweaters to keep warm. My nose always seemed to be cold, too.

Several years ago we decided to heat our home with a wood-burning stove, and have never regretted it, although it took some talking and persuasion on my husband's part to get me to endorse the idea. But two words helped: warmth and cheap.

There were a few things he didn't tell me about wood-burning, however, so I'll share what I've learned:

After buying the stove, which will cost between $200 and $1,500 or more, you will need to buy stove pipe, which costs about $15 a foot - probably more by now. You'll need a chain saw for cutting wood, and after the first season's practice cutting, it'll burn out and you'll need a new one.

The next purchase should be a smoke alarm - perhaps that should be the first purchase - several alarms, in fact. They set a person's mind at ease. They're good wake-up alarms for when the wind rises, as happened last week, dies down, changes direction or ceases altogether; or fog, rain, snow or sleet occur. The weather and barometric conditions can cause a phenomenon called a downdraft. The stove will emit little puffs of smoke out the front damper. (A damper is something that controls the flow of air into the stove - there are two of them, one in the stove pipe and one on the stove door - the manipulation of dampers can take on the form of regulating a thermonuclear reactor.) Smoke will also puff out around the stove door, the seams around the stove pipe or billow out any other cranny or crevice. The smoke will enter the smoke detector, setting off the alarm usually around two or three in the morning.

The alarm could wake a dead person or cause a live person's heart to stop. You jump out of bed and quickly look around and determine what set off the alarm, and pull out the battery to shut it up. Stumbling to the front door, you open it to allow fresh Arctic air in and then go to the stove to fiddle with the dampers to get the smoking to stop.

After the frightened kids are back in bed, the house is aired out, the dog has stopped barking, the battery is back in the alarm and you're back in bed trying to get warm, pick a fight with the person who wanted a wood stove.

On the day that the house is at its cleanest, that's the day the ashes will be cleaned out of the stove. In the process a fine ash will settle on newly-vacuumed rugs, floors, upholstery and drapes. Anyone who has freshly shampooed hair will want to put on a cap or hat to cover it.

There will be ashes around the stove. Do not be tempted to vacuum them. A vacuum cleaner will suck up a teeny tiny live coal which will become a tempest inside the cleaner, and before you know it, smoke is pouring out the vacuum exhaust, the dust bag is on fire and the vacuum cleaner is quickly hurled out the front door never to work the same again. And the smoke alarm goes off.

While you're at it, don't forget to clean the stove pipe and chimney, too. If you don't it gets all cruddy and sooty and VERY combustible. It will eventually catch fire, trust me. The noise and smell of a chimney fire is so scary you'll call the fire department. The fire will probably be out before they arrive and you'll feel like an idiot for panicking, but you'll do the same thing the next time there's a fire. And there WILL be a next time.

Be prepared for several visits from your insurance agent. He is VERY interested in wood -burning stoves. You may even find that your homeowner's insurance has been canceled. Look around for another agent and company, in that case.

Wood heat is a very dry heat. Prepare for dry, itchy skin, static electricity and furniture that cracks and/or falls apart. Lotion will take care of the skin, and a humidifier will take care of the rest. UNLESS you have hard water, in which case the humidifier will turn into one large hunk of lime and shuck out its insides within a week.

If this happens, a large coffee can or some other container could be filled with water and placed on the stove to provide moisture in the air. This will cause the windows to fog up and frost over, only to melt and drip down into the sill starting a process called wood rot.

The owners of a wood-burning stove will begin a new game. It's called, "last one to go to bed has to bank the fire." To bank a fire for the night you must fill the stove with plenty of wood and have the dampers set just right so the fire is burning enough to heat, but not enough to burn all the wood in the night. Waking up in the early morning to a cold house and a dead fire is not conducive to domestic harmony.

And yet with all the mess and inconvenience, I wouldn't trade my woodburner for anything.

It's the only thing in the house that keeps me warm and doesn't have sharp toenails.

The Old Swimmin' Hole

The family at play.

Listed among the assets of country living is handy access to the humble farm pond. I can think of few things as refreshing as a swim in the pond at the end of a long, sweat-drenched, hot, sultry summer day.

A really good swimming pond, ideally, should not be a livestock pond. A stock pond on a hot muggy day, while better than nothing at all, can be pretty messy.

No, I'm referring to a fenced-from-livestock, old-fashioned pond.

The nicest swimming ponds are those that have had loads of sand brought in to make a nice mud-free beach, and preferably they have some kind of dock or diving area, but those aren't altogether necessary.

Come along with me, if you will, to our pond where we'll go and cool off after a day of working in hay, canning green beans, commuting to work in the city, playing or just fiddlin' around.

We'll walk a short distance thought a hay field where chiggers may invade a person's privacy; and if barefooted, you'll step on the one thistle in 30 acres hidden down in the alfalfa, but no matter....

Before last summer when, against Bob's advice, I grabbed a pair of wire cutters, there used to be fence around the pond. It was a woven wire fence, topped with barbed wire where a person risked a ripped-open artery just to climb over it to gain access to the pond. Following my assault on the fence, which Bob now agrees was a wise decision, entrance to the pond is as simple as walking into a yard.

After entering the pond enclosure, stop and take a deep breath. Smell the air with the scents of clover in bloom and the neighbor's fresh-cut hay. Look at the placid, still water, dimpled here and there by water bugs or perhaps a fish surfacing. That is, unless you've brought the kids along, in which case they're already in the water and swimming halfway across the pond, a water fight is in progress, and one of the littlest has water in her nose and doesn't like it one bit.

Since this pond hasn't yet had a load of sand or pea gravel, you'll cautiously enter the water, slipping and sliding in the gooey muck with some of the gumbo oozing up between your toes. The pond water creeps up and up ....until one mighty plunge takes care of getting the rest of you wet.

You scoot off and leave the shallow, knee-deep water behind as you head to the deeper and clearer water and, oh heaven and bliss, the feeling of all's right with the world as you roll over and float on your back, sniff the loamy smell of pond water, and watch the clouds overhead, while the kids continue to splash and play on the other side of the pond.

Soon you'll be persuaded to swim over to a floating dock the boys have just recently completed. They're awful proud of it and well they should be. It's made from 2 x 8s, 1 x 12s, sheets of foam sheathing, discarded porch carpet and about six thousand nails of varying sizes. The dock probably weighs half a ton dry, and how they got it from the garage to the pond with only a riding mower and its little cart remains a mystery, but they got the job done. And now they're wanting to show off its good points such as neatness and buoyancy, and they wait impatiently for praise of the design, engineering and building skills going into the dock - praise that is soon forthcoming.

Try getting on the dock. Try real hard.

If you're a little out of shape, you'll puff and pant, groan and grunt, but eventually you'll be able to get your knee up on the dock and soon you'll be able to bring up the rest of you. There you'll be, looking out over the world from your floating perch, then a teenage boy will join you, then another, and the neighbor boy, too, will nimbly climb up.

A little bump, the corner of the dock dips, a nudge, a push and over the side a boy goes and then another. You discover you're about to participate in a game of "King of the Dock," and you suddenly forget you dislike getting water in your nose, that you're at least 20 pounds overweight, you've got arthritis in the knees and elbows and you're approaching middle age.

You forget all that and push off a 15-year-old muscled youth and feel real good about it. Another thing you feel is a hand around your ankle (you forgot to watch behind you!) and ultimately the feel of pond water closing around your head. You gain access to the surface only to see 95 pounds of a 13-year-old waving his arms around, trying to keep his balance on the dock, but he knows, and you know, that soon he's going to land on top of you if you don't get out of there - fast!

Go over to the pond edge to tread water and catch your breath and - what was that? You've felt the first of the pond-things. "Things" range from anything like a slimy old cattail being mistaken for a snake (in your mind it is probably poisonous, certainly large) to a rock being mistaken for a toe-grabbing snapping turtle, or mud splatters for leeches.

You hurriedly swim to deeper water where the prospect of wearing out, sinking and drowning is more appealing than the idea of being touched, bitten, scratched or fondled by any of the "things" imagination has conjured up.

All too soon, the sun is setting and the air has become cooler. Lightning bugs are popping out and barn swallows are swooping down to the pond's surface. It's time to go back to the house.

Didn't we have a good time together?

Mosaic in bark. *photo by Bob Nandell*

Memories Of Trees

It was a crisp fall Saturday morning when I heard the sound of the chain saw near the house.

"Mom, have you seen what Dad's doing?" exclaimed an agitated daughter as she burst in the door. "Are you gonna let him?"

What "Dad was doing" was cutting down a dying elm tree which had been littering our yard with falling limbs and branches for ages.

There had been talk about cutting it down for years, but as with any other such talk of taking away any of my trees, the talk ceased abruptly when I was around.

You see, I love trees - any and all trees, and it nearly tears at my soul to see any destroyed or injured.

This particular elm tree wasn't even real old. In fact, my brother had noted that it was an eyesore, and not old enough to be really large and beautiful, so why didn't I just cut it down, he wondered.

"That's Grandpa's tree," I said. And after I explained the story of the tree to him, he said simply, "Leave it alone, then."

It was 1970 when the tree was just a sprout, a mere whip of an elm tree. We were living in a mobile home on the site we would someday build our house. We had two small boys and another baby was on the way.

My grandparents and my mother were visiting us and it was my grandpa's habit to walk around the place, inspect it, and make suggestions on everything from barn paint to fence wire to cutting out worthless sprouts of junk trees. Grandpa was walking with his cane - he would have been around 82 by then - and as he was walking past the boys' swing set, he used his cane to beat down the elm sprout which had sprung up near it.

"Dirty trees, these elms. You should kill it out now," And he continued his leisurely Sunday afternoon stroll around the place.

The little elm tree was beaten down for a while, but sprung back twice as hardy and over the next couple of decades it weathered other adversities besides my grandpa's cane.

There were hail storms, ice storms, droughts, wind storms and a tornado. It was also a climbing tree for small boys and later their two little sisters. It took several batterings and dropped large limbs, littering the ground with sticks and branches, but still it lingered.

Half of it had been trimmed out a few years ago following a bad wind storm which broke off a major limb, so the tree was looking kind of ratty and lop-sided. But I kept insisting, when the subject would arise, that the tree was healthy enough and in the corner of the back yard, so it wasn't like it was going to fall over on a car or an electric line or anything.

But the summer's constant wet and soggy ground caused the tree to begin looking very dead in several different areas. Limbs fell even with no wind to push them out of the tree.

Cut it or not to cut it? Sentiment told me no. I could still in my mind's eye see my grandpa out there beating down the little whip of a sprout with his hickory cane. I still treasure the photograph I have of him, taken a few minutes later, as he playfully decided to show us he could swing on the boys' swing and did a pretty good job of it much to the little boys' delight and merriment. The snapshot shows his feet leaving the ground and his legs going up into the air while his jaunty fedora is tipped cockily on his head.

Ah well, memories. It would have to go, I thought. "But I don't want to see it when you do cut it down," I warned Bob.

He cut it down on a sunny morning when our oldest son was home for a visit and was helping his dad.

Our son came in the house after the job was done and you would have thought someone had just killed the family pet. And in a way, that's what had happened.

"What's going on around here?" he asked. "I thought we never got rid of trees!"

And that's the way it's always been. Our family has always treasured trees. There's rarely a year that goes by when we don't plant at least one. Slowly over the years Bob's gifts to me have changed. Now instead of getting me lacy underwear or cookbooks, he gets me trees; once a blue spruce, last year weeping willows.

The kids are tree-nuts, too. One summer when the county came to cut down a few trees alongside the road, I heard about it from one of the boys telling a friend, "Yeah, they're some guys cutting trees by our place. When Mom finds out about it, she'll have a fit.

I've loved trees since I was a little girl. My brother and I made treehouses and we swung from tree branches. Our rope swing was hung from the arm of a large maple tree. He played trucks and cars under one tree; I had my playhouse under another. A large towering spruce tree in our front yard could be seen from the town square four miles away. Now those trees are gone, bulldozed or blown down. And when they went so did a precious part of my childhood.

I know that I must have instilled some of my love of trees in the kids because of what one of my sons said is his most favorite memory. He was at a Boy Scout campout in Stephens State Forest when he climbed a pine tree and laid across some of its feathery boughs and went to sleep to the sound of the breeze blowing and the gentle rocking motion of the tree. He said that was the most peaceful place he'd ever been in his life. I agree. Outside of a mother's arms, there's no more peaceful place on God's earth than by a tree.

When we moved to Warren County that spring of 1970, there was a homely yet sturdy cedar tree windbreak which still protects our home. The other mature trees included elm trees and a large pine tree - all of them sort of stunted-looking on one side because of damage from the fire which had destroyed the house that had stood on the place years and years before.

We added trees over the years - mostly soft maples, since they could be found nearby and were hardy, not to mention free. A clump birch was planted, grew to maturity, got chewed on by a teen-age son's horse, withered and died.

An ash tree was planted on a summer morning in 1974 while the little boys were still sleeping. I had gotten it on clearance at K-Mart and planted it one morning to keep my hands busy and to keep from crying. Bob had just left for a three-week-long postal training school in Oklahoma, and I would be alone with our three little boys. The place had seemed suddenly very lonely as he had driven away.

The trees are our friends in the summer with shade and coolness, and keep us company in the winter with the sounds of creaking, ice-covered limbs, and flakes of frost and snow glinting in the light of day. They surround us with gold in the fall when the leaves change color. The trees provide a sancuary for the hundreds of songbirds in dozens of species which nest in our trees.

It might sound as if our trees are members of the family, and in a way I guess they are, loved and protected as any cherished family member would be for as long as we can hold onto them.

Tim and his snapping turtle.

The Joy Of Cleaning Turtles

If a woman has a sensitive nature and a queasy stomach, she has no business living on a farm, or more to the point, raising sons. Fortunately, I'm not real sensitive, and my stomach, with the help of Rolaids, has grown considerably less squeamish in recent years.

In a week's time it seems that most local species of Mother Nature's array of creepy, crawly, slimy critters have been hooked, caught, snared or grabbed around here.

The first creature brought in for my inspection was a crawdad. The Cajuns of Louisiana may find these bug-eyed, clawed, ugly little monsters a delicacy for cooking. I prefer to have them left where they were meant to be - in a God-forsaken, alligator-infested swamp in the south, or at the very least in the next township. Instead we have the thing being used to chase a little girl screaming and in tears, or to sucker a brother into placing a finger or toe in the creature's pincers.

It was getting dark one evening when the youngest fisherboy came in with his catch, a large catfish. The rest of the menfolk were gone and he needed help cleaning the fish. I hadn't cleaned a catfish since I was maybe 12, and all I remembered was that they have a sharp fin to be wary of, and that there is skin to be removed, not scales.

I told him to get the head off and then I'd help with the rest. He came in a short while later and said the head was "almost off," but the fish kept wiggling. Wiggling? Omigosh, I had forgotten to tell him to kill the fish first.

I ran out, saw the situation and grabbed a 2 x 4 and sent a soul rocketing to fish heaven. The animal rights-people would have been unhappy, but Robbie was satisfied.

We could find no pliers with which to skin the fish, so we made do with a dull paring knife and fingers. "Boy, Mom," my son said in admiration, "You're pretty good at this. You must've done this when you were a little kid a long time ago."

I had hardly gotten the odor of fish off my hands when the next evening the boys brought in a big, old bait-snatching turtle. They thought they'd beaten it to death with a rock until a long-clawed turtle foot whipped out and snared a filthy, mud-encrusted shirttail. Bravery vanished. I looked at the size of the turtle and figured it had crawled out of the primeval depths of some slough around the time the Wright Brothers were checking out wind directions at Kitty Hawk.

I'd always heard that turtle meat is delicious, and by the size of this monster, it should yield a lot. But I didn't know how to go about dressing it. I looked in my "Joy of Cooking" cookbook. It has a lot of strange and generally useless information. I knew I'd struck out when I read, "Sea turtles attain a huge size...."

But I read on to see how one would handle a sea turtle and translated that into an Iowa snapping turtle. From what I could understand, you were supposed to boil the whole thing, shell, feet, tail, insides (gasp!) - the whole thing and THEN dress it. That might be fine if I had a nice seashore handy, a very large pot and a bonfire, but not in my kitchen!

A couple of phone calls to neighbors yielded little information except to be wary of the jaws of a "dead" turtle. I then had my son go out and dispatch the turtle head.

I hesitate to go into the quite gory details of dressing a turtle, but I'll give some advice to those tempted to act as turtle butchers.

Turtle skin is closely akin to the best of Samsonite luggage, tougher even. The sharpest, pointiest knife bounced off.

Just because the turtle no longer has a head doesn't mean that he's still not "alive." It's a very eerie feeling to be working on the leg part of a long-dead turtle and then feel the leg move. You will probably do as I did by immediately jumping back and making a little noise like a scream. Your kids will laugh and snicker at you, but you will notice that they're keeping a safe distance away.

As the sun sets, plenty of mosquitoes, gnats and flies will come and land on you and nibble away. You will slap at them and leave a bloody, fishy-smelling, sticky handprint for the insects to feast on. (You also notice your helpers have deserted you, and are indoors watching The Dukes of Hazzard.)

You'll finally give up with knives and supplement them with an arsenal which includes a sledge hammer, chisel and hacksaw.

About two hours later when you're done sawing, hacking, carving, slicing, pulling, tearing, and skinning, you'll find yourself with maybe a pound or two of turtle meat to cook. At least you hope its the eatable turtle meat, and not something else, such as its... uh....er...reproductive-type organs.

After I had cleaned up, and had the meat soaking in salt water, I wondered what I'd do with it. I decided to cook it in the pressure cooker, and it smelled so good. It should. I'd read somewhere that turtle meat is like seven varieties of meat: Pork, beef, chicken, and others which Midwesterners have probably never tasted, nor would want to.

But I was left to wonder what to do with the cooked turtle meat. Boil some macaroni and have turtle goulash? Turtle, tomato and lettuce sandwiches? Turtle and noodles? Turtle loaf?

I'm wondering, of course, how to prepare it for the rest of the family. With my vivid memory of a dark and bloody evening and squirming flesh, I think I'll opt for a balony sandwich.

No Water

We had a long mid-winter three-day weekend ahead of us, and the girls were out of school as well. We were looking forward to our time together; we would all do something special together, we thought.

As it turned out, we did.

It was the first day of that long weekend when I was getting ready to make lunch and turned on the kitchen faucet. Nothing. My heart sank. "My God. We're out of water," I said forlornly.

All talking and motion ceased in the house. For a moment our lives stood still as we each digested what the words "no water" conveyed. To the girls it meant no showers and no shampooing hair, and some of the more unpleasant facts of life must be faced when it comes to dealing with sanitary facilities or lack of them.

For me, it meant no laundry can be done; dishes are washed by hand in about a quart of water and rinsed with a pint-full. There's no miracle-faucet to fill the coffee maker, or to wet a dish cloth to wipe up a spill, or even to water the plants unless it comes out of a jug, and that is so unhandy. Then there's also the fact that I, too, like a shower, and enjoy washing my hair, and yes, even shaving my legs.

Bob thinks of no water, and knows he's in for the long hard work of diagnosing the cause and repairing our rural water system. And these things never occur in 60 degree weather, oh my no. On this day, it was three degrees and the ground was a skating rink of ice.

Of the two of us, I don't know who had the more intolerable and uncomfortable situation. Bob, as he toiled outside in such frigid weather, or me having to listen to our teen-aged daughters gripe, "My hair is so oily-looking, and I feel so gross....when's Dad going to have the water running again?"

While Bob wearily donned his insulated coveralls, I gathered up gallon jugs and some buckets to hold the water we'd have to get at the neighbor's.

Many people today aren't acquainted with even the most minimal information on rural water, REAL rural water; that is, water pumped from a farm well as opposed to Rural Water piped in from a far-away municipal water system.

Those of us who live in the country and have a well to depend upon as a water supply have never taken water or its purity for granted.

When we first moved to our place in Warren County, we planned to use the water from the well that had furnished household water to other owners of the rural property we'd purchased. True, the house it had once supplied had long since burned down, and cattle had been fed in the area for several years, but we figured the well would supply us with a steady supply of drinkable water.

I was wrong on all counts. The well and its contents had not been used for many years, and whole dynasties of bacteria known as e.coli had been created in the murky depths of the 65-foot deep well. This type of bacteria is usually caused by organic waste that can be found in anything from decaying autumn leaves to the occasional rabbit carelessly hippity-hopping along until it plops in between loose boards covering the well and meets its sad, yet hairy end at the bottom; or e.coli can come from (gasp!) feedlot waste from the nearby cattle, washed in from rainfall or draining off in ground water.

The happy note is coliform bacteria is the type which can be destroyed by boiling the water before drinking it. Knowing all the things that caused coliform bacteria, however, I wouldn't have touched the water for more than mopping floors if it'd been boiled for a month.

We cleansed the well by pouring jugs of chlorine bleach down the well, pumping it dry and letting it fill again. Then we tested the water once more and found it no longer contained coliform bacteria.

There was something else in the water, though, which we couldn't do a thing about. Nitrates. Our water was declared unsafe to drink because of nitrates, and it probably is unsafe to this day. Oh, adults can drink it, and we do - have for years with no side effects, but pregnant women and children under age one can't drink it. When we first moved onto the farm, we had both conditions to contend with; we had a child under one, and, I blushingly admit, I was pregnant with our third child. All those conditions would reappear a few years later with our fourth and fifth children arriving at unseemly regular intervals.

We began regular routines of getting city water from Bob's parents in Des Moines. During the times I, or whatever baby was around at the time, couldn't drink farm water, we had the city water to rely on.

The thing about nitrates is you can't boil it out of the water or treat the water in anyway I've ever heard of. Unlike coliform, boiling makes the nitrate condition worse, it concentrates it.

So regular water-testing has been a part of our household routine like getting booster shots or doing income taxes. We fill the little bottle up with a water sample, put it in its foam container and ship it out to Iowa City, and await test results.

And that steady supply of water I first mentioned?

Only the truly foolish or fresh-from-the-city would ever depend on a farm well as a bottomless water source.

There are the dry years when even the most dependable wells dry up or supply such a paltry trickle of water that family lifestyles are altered. Entertaining decreases or ceases altogether; the coin laundry in town is used regularly instead of the family washer in the basement. Lawns are never watered and flower beds are watered sparingly, at best, and usually not at all. Arguments and hot words erupt over the length of showers taken by teen-agers. Stern lectures on conserving water are regular fare whenever water is discovered being wasted or is allowed to run full force down the drain as someone waits for hot water or colder water.

That first well I referred to may have been 65-feet deep, but it was only about 11 inches wide - and that does not make a whole lot of water to use. In fact, if more than five gallons were used at one time, the water level would fall below the electric pump and the pump would have to be shut off, or it would burn out. Pumping equipment is expensive, incidentally, and not simple to install. The well would usually fill up overnight, but still it was a worrisome nuisance. Fortunately, we had another well on our property, a wide, deep well, that we eventually had connected to the house.

And that is the well which was not providing us with water on that icy, frigid February day we had all looked forward to.

I don't understand water-pumping or pressure systems enough to explain them, except its a heavy, wet and slippery job pulling the heavy pump and all the pipe 75-feet or so from the depths of the well.

First, though, Bob had to get the heavy concrete lid off the well using a lift on the tractor. Except the tractor battery was dead; he found the battery was also dead in the beat-up old Mazda pickup, and finally had to jump-start the tractor using the family car.

By this time he was cold and feeling extremely frustrated and hadn't even begun to work on the well. The wind was picking up and it had begun to sleet. It was a miserable day.

With the lid finally off the well, we could look down into it, and see that there was water at least; that meant the problem was the pump. I hate working over an uncovered well. I feel like I'm getting pulled into it, or will fall in it, or at the very least, my glasses will fall from my face and be lost to the dark depths. It's always when we're working over an open well, that the family pooch decides it wants to be near us, or the cats begin winding themselves around our legs. Then I'm afraid they'll either knock us into the drink, or fall in themselves, and wouldn't that be a mess? And not to put too fine a line on it, standing next to an open well is probably not the best place for a wife to be if she begins to make unsolicited suggestions about possible causes of the water pump failure, or whines about the cold and her wet hands, while her husband is testing fuses, wiring and wrestling with a 100-pound water pump.

I noticed an electrical box - a control box of some sort laying on the ground after Bob had removed it from the pole near the well. In the box I noticed a cylindrical object, a capacitor it's called, looking like a Roman candy after the 4th of July, as if the bottom had been blown out of it. There were distinct soot marks near it. I don't know much about electricity, but I do know that burn and soot marks are bad signs.

I casually asked Bob if he'd been wearing his glasses while he worked. And he admitted no, he hadn't - hadn't wanted to fool with them, and maybe have them drop off and fall in the well.

In an off-hand manner, I directed his attention to the box and the soot mark. "Well, I'll be damned," he said, relieved at finding the cause of the problem. And I felt so proud of myself, and so smug. But also smart enough not to remind him if he'd worn his glasses he'd have noticed the marks, then he wouldn't have had to do all the work outside or remove the top from the well, or pull up the pump or jump-start the tractor or any of it.

No, I didn't say any of those things. There are times a woman wants to appear intelligent and on-the-ball and have her spouse praise her. And then there are times a woman instinctively knows that the time is not good to remind, second-guess or gloat. And definitely not when there is an open well four feet away.

He soon had the electrical problem fixed, the pump and the pipe were lowered into the well, the lid placed on it and we once again had running water. Showers could be taken, and hair shampooed. Dishes were stacked in the dishwasher and the laundry pile diminished. Wilting plants were watered and ice cube trays filled. Contentment with our life in the country reigned once again.

And we had another reminder of one of life's lessons: Never take an unending, steady-flowing supply of water for granted outside the city limits.

Two-Legged Snakes And Weasels

It was early Saturday morning, a time of sleeping-in in my household. But I was awake already, and it was only 5:15.

When I'd gone to bed the evening before, the weather had been icy and sleety with warnings of hazardous road conditions. Was it still that way, I sleepily wondered? Or had the weather changed and the weatherman been proved wrong? Again.

I reached an arm out of the blankets and hit the on-button of the nearby radio, and in the dark tried to tune it in to anything that had central Iowa weather on it. To turn on a light to see the dial would have meant to search also for my glasses in order to actually be able to read the dial, and that activity might awaken my sleeping spouse. I continued to troll around on the dial for the Clear-Channel Voice of the Middle West, WHO-Radio in Des Moines.

Too far on the dial one way and I'd hear a preacher in Oklahoma; too far the other way and I'd end up with lots of static and run off the dial completely.

"....MEAN MEN! I mean these guys are jerks of the first water!" I heard, as a familiar-sounding voice grated out the angry words over the airwaves.

Bingo. I'd found my station, but what was this I was listening to? That voice....where had I heard it?

Ah ha! Of course. Tom Snyder of late-night TV programs. Tom Snyder, the subject of the delightful parody by Dan Ackroyd on "Saturday Night Live," where Snyder is portrayed as a cross between Morton Downey Jr. and Dan Rather.

And now here he'd landed as a talk-show host on a call-in radio show based in Los Angeles.

The subject of his diatribe appeared to be mean people, specifically people in management; powerful people who seem to delight in being nasty, mean-spirited, conniving, back-stabbing, cretinous jerks.

Oh, those kind of people! I'd heard of the type, and even met a few, I thought, as I lay in the dark listening to him rave on in outrage.

He mentioned the names of the three meanest men he'd ever worked for or with. They were TV network executives, so naturally the names meant little to me. Still, his descriptions of some of their unsavory and calculating sadistic actions drew a sympathetic response from me. I'd been told of similar behavior by people in positions of power.

The types of men he was referring to as jerks I usually call snakes or weasels, which really is to malign reptiles or small furry mammals, although I have other names I can use to describe unpleasant types.

Snyder's final word on the three men he'd mentioned was that he hoped they got what they deserved.

"....but I don't wish them ill," he said.

No, of course not, Tom.

He then quoted a line from the movie, "Network News," where a network exec remorselessly and mercilessly fires an employee and then makes an insincere offer, ".....But if there's ever anything I can do for you, just let me know...." To which the employee answers, "Well, I hope you die soon."

I lay there in the early morning with the radio turned down to a murmur and listened to Snyder's remarks about mean people and thought of the stories I've heard of weaselly snakes who are over-ambitious and cruel, completely thoughtless of others, whose main aim in life is protecting and furthering their own careers and ambitions, while keeping their tails covered; who would feed their own mothers to the wolves for recognition or a promotion.

These sorts cause heartache, heartburn, migraines, loss of appetite, irritability, depression, untold stress, sometimes tragedy, and often the loss of good employees who finally give up and leave their jobs to find a less hostile environment in which to work.

In another time, these meanies would've been horse-whipped, put in stocks or worse. These days they're promoted, carrying out the famous or infamous Peter Principle, "Rising to the level of their own incompetence," as they've shoved their way up the corporate ladder, climbing over countless bodies and unhappy souls in the process.

My attention turned to the radio show as Snyder wound down his program by once again mentioning his list of three mean men.

Then came a voice from the other pillow beside me. "I could add another name to that list," my husband said.

And we began laughing together as we recalled the sudden transfer of a former nemesis, someone considered mean and power-nasty, in what is sometimes called "a lateral promotion," a fancy-sounding phrase which often means getting a person out of an immediate area long enough to quiet things down, before a full-scale mutiny or worse occurs.

And we rejoiced in the truth of another little nugget of justness which sometimes happens on the side of right, and that is: What goes around, comes around. Simply stated, eventually they'll get theirs.

But we don't wish them ill.

Of course not.

Iowa Christmas, brrrrr! *photo by Bob Nandell*

Real Weather, Winter Edition

The forecast a couple of weeks ago for bitterly cold, sub-zero temperatures with the added threat of dangerously low wind-chill levels was disheartening to hear.

I decided to pay little attention to the forecast, however, since our weather forecasters have an increasingly frequent tendency to be wrong. Not just a shade wrong, but totally screwed-up wrong. One of the more recent examples occurred on the very day the mega-technical and highly-touted, super-accurate, colorful Doppler radar system was going on line at a Des Moines television station. That was to be the day, the television weatherman said, we would have a serious snowstorm.

People got blizzard-mania and crowded into grocery stores to get essentials like toilet paper, batteries, milk, disposable diapers and beer. Meetings, athletic events and party plans were called off for the evening as people were advised to go home, stay there and keep off the roads.

The weather stayed clear and we didn't receive any snow.

The next morning in an attempt to put a positive spin on the weather forecast goof-up, the TV station's early morning smiley-face greeted us with the news that Iowans had received a late Christmas present when a predicted snowstorm failed to develop. That was a different way to look at it, I thought. She could just as well have said we had an early Valentine's present.

I was grumpy and felt disappointed and let down when I looked out the window that morning and saw the same stark and unattractive landscape as the day before. I actually had looked forward to a nice blanketing of snow. I wanted to say to the Doppler fans and techno-droids: Return to the old ways of weather prediction - look out the window! Or read the Farmer's Almanac. Just get it right for a change.

A couple of weeks ago they did just that when the predicted Siberian Express cold wave struck. The thing that surprised me about the whole thing was the closing of schools for cold weather.

"What?" I exclaimed when I heard the announcement. "Closing schools? Why? Kids are becoming the biggest bunch of whiners and wimps I've ever seen! Or is it the teachers? Or parents?"

My husband, Mr. School Board Member and I've-Heard-It-All-type guy, explained to me that it was so awful cold that a school building would be hard to keep comfortably warm with the temperature outside at 25 below. Also, he said acidly, parents would raise hell because their darlings might be expected to go out in the cold, while the rest of us were scraping frost from the car windows and donning extra pairs of socks to head for work.

I really had scant sympathy with any of that, and it all goes back to my own childhood, which is more often than not taking on the aura of "the good old days."

When I was a kid we had cold winters, too. Not as cold as today, certainly, because the "wind-chill factor" had not been invented to make temperatures sound and feel colder. If it was 20-below in 1954 with a 30-mile per hour wind, it was still only 20-below. Period. No 80-below wind-chill factor figured into it. The only factor the wind played was that you kept your back to it if you were a little kid walking to or from school. I spent a lot of my kidhood days walking backward as did a lot of others.

It was about two miles to the country school my brother and I and our cousins, who lived next door, attended. When I was six, I remember walking to school in all kinds of weather. And when I was in third grade, my five-year-old brother entered school and was expected to walk with the rest of us.

Oh it was cold, all right. But we were dressed for it; sweaters and heavy winter coats and stocking hats, scarves and gloves and mittens and long pants and long underwear. We had uninsulated rubber boots we HAD to wear. It wasn't until we entered high school that we considered them uncool and wore them only until we got out of the parental line of vision and onto the frigid school bus where we would rip them off, refusing to be seen in them. We preferred instead wet and cold, freezing feet.

But on that long walk to grade school, when we would duck under the bridge at Blackbird Creek to catch our breaths, then venture across the ice just for fun, then clamber back to the road, we would only rarely get a ride to school. And then only if someone could get their car started and had chains on the tires, or the roads were cleared. But the cars were never warm since heaters seldom worked.

Burdened by heavy, bulky clothes, we shuffled along to school, and by the time we got there, having sampled the depth of snowdrifts, or stopped to make snow angels on the way, our boots would be packed with snow, our cotton socks would have slid down our heels into a wet wad in our shoes and there would be a distinct line of chapped skin about mid-way up our calves where our boots had slapped against the backs of our legs.

At school after we had poured the snow from our boots and pulled up our wet socks, we would set our boots near the stove to dry them out before the walk back home. Cold, wet boots are extremely uncomfortable.

The school was heated by a coal stove and the littlest kids sat nearest the stove with the older students taking turns getting up to warm themselves by the stove. Recesses were sometimes spent outdoors if our clothes had dried out enough during the morning; otherwise, we stayed in and played games.

The school day over, older kids helped little kids on with their heavy clothes, and we retraced our route of that morning.

Once at home, many of us had farm chores which included chopping openings in pond ice or pumping water for livestock, throwing out hay to livestock, gathering any eggs before they froze and cracked, bringing in coal or wood, and milking cows.

Then after chores and supper we could settle down to an evening of listening to the radio shows while doing math problems on an oil cloth-covered kitchen table, working on a jigsaw puzzle with Mama, and in later years watching Andy Griffith, Red Skelton or Wagon Train on television.

The more I recall those days, even with the hard work and discomfort, the more dear they seem to me.

Winterscape on the Banger farm. *photo by Bob Nandell*

Country-Style Winter Weather

With the recent blizzards and sub-sub-zero temperatures falling to 40-below -God knows what the wind-chill was - we Iowans can be proud of our endurance to such rigors.

I read or heard somewhere that there are hotter temperatures in the world (the Sahara) than Iowa reaches in the summer, and there are colder temperatures (the Arctic) than Iowa falls to in the winter, but nowhere in the world does it reach both the high temperatures and the lows in one place as it does here in the Hawkeye State. I'm grasping, I suppose, for a positive view of living in the Midwest in the winter.

The blizzard of a few weeks ago brought back memories of other bad winter storms we have known. In our household, we were remembering the blizzard of April, 1973. We had just moved upstairs into our still-unfinished house after living in the basement for two years. I well remember that blizzard since it was one of the rare times Bob did not make it home from work - he was more or less stranded in Des Moines. At the time, we had three small boys.

Usually I enjoy winter storms, but only if me and mine are at home and accounted for. That is the one prerequisite. My kids - most of them now grown and away from home - recall with fondness the times we have been snowed in - all of us. The soup kettle was always on and there was always a Monopoly game or some other pursuit in progress. If the electricity went off, oil lamps were brought out and we enjoyed a "pioneer" evening. One reason I've always insisted on a gas kitchen range - not for me electric or ceramic top - is the fact that we can enjoy heat from the oven and hot food, uninterrupted by the cessation of electricity.

Perhaps the winter I was 14 is the worst I ever remember. I was a kid in Missouri when that storm struck. As I recall, we were out of school for a week or more because of it. The storm struck on a day my 12-year-old brother was home sick, complaining of a belly ache.

The day had started with freezing rain and changed to a snowstorm. My brother's stomach ache never improved and in fact worsened during the day. Personally, I was unconcerned about it all, considering him a whiner and a baby, after all. That is, until my mom called the doctor - something that only once before had been done and that was when I was 12 and had a bad stomach ache. That time, Dr. Mac came to our farm during a thunderstorm, walked down our mud lane and carried me in his arms back to his car to take me to the hospital where he later operated on me for appendicitis.

But it was my brother who was sick this time when Mama called the doctor and was told to bring him to the hospital. When she tried, the car slid on the ice and into the ditch as soon as she pulled out of our driveway. My Uncle Kenneth, who lived across the field, was recruited to help. He could do anything, including putting chains on his car and driving my mom and brother into town in the middle of a snowstorm.

That was the last time I saw my mom and brother for more than a week. He had a ruptured appendix, and my mom stayed at the hospital with him since he was not recovering too well from the surgery. Not that she would have had any choice. Blowing snow filled the air for days, and all the roads were closed by huge drifts.

I was on the farm alone, feeling quite grown up at 14, and in charge of feeding and watering a couple dozen bred ewes, our milk cows, taking care of chickens and watching the water pipes from freezing. In those days of coal-burning, I fed the old stove and carried out ashes. But as the days passed after the blizzard, I wasn't feeling quite so grown up. I missed my mom, and yes, even my whiny brother.

There are still clippings in our family archives (which is really an old shoe box) showing newspaper photographs of the aftermath of that snowstorm; photos of snow piles as high as the second floor of the Putnam County Courthouse.

Mostly, though, when I think of winter time and storms, of blizzards and being prepared, I'm always drawn to the book I read as a school girl, "The Long Winter," by Laura Ingalls Wilder. Perhaps it was reading that book when I was a young girl that gave me my hoarding instincts for winter when I had a family of my own to look after.

In the book, which dealt with what I figure was the record-breaking winter of 1886, the Ingalls family ran out of coal and wood for their stove and were reduced to twisting bundles of slough hay into fuel. They ran out of flour and no trains or shipments could get through because of snow, so they ground wheat in a coffee grinder to make a coarse bread or sometimes a gruel.

I've also had the stories told to me by my mother of the winter of 1936, I believe it was, a horrible winter. She remembers walking to her small rural school that winter. (School was not called off because of weather or cold temperatures in those days, nor in the days I attended that same school years later.) My mom has told me that you could not tell where the road or the ditch or the fence lines were - the tops of fence posts were covered by snow. Her snow memories always impressed me. But along with that, it was Laura Ingalls Wilder and her story of "The Long Winter" that always has me preparing around October for the worst that winter can throw at us.

The weather forecasters and soothsayers have been wringing their hands this winter that the Greenhouse Effect and the Vanishing Ozone Layer are having an effect on our weather patterns - that's why we had the horribly cold weather earlier and the record-breaking snowfalls all over the country.

Winter weather patterns have not changed - an environmental Armageddon is not at hand. Mother Nature is reverting back to the winters of a few years ago.

We had become soft and complacent to have forgotten them.

photo by Bob Nandell

Cutting Firewood

I went on a family wood-cutting mission on a recent late autumn afternoon, something I hadn't done in years.

One of the things I miss now that my sons are grown and away from home is the work they once performed - such as getting out in the cold and pursuing manly tasks with their dad - male-bonding it's called nowadays. I find myself often called upon to do that same work now.

Not that I didn't help cut wood for our main heating source, a wood-burning stove, when the boys were home, but when I helped I would do it on mild winter days. On really cold days when Bob announced that a wood-cutting trip was being planned, "It's a fine day to be outside! The work will keep us warm!" he would say with enthusiasm, I could find something more urgent that needed my attention in the house. Or I would feign an approaching cold or flu, or sometimes stoop to making a vague reference to something "female" which would cause my sons to quickly flee while suggesting I stay inside.

And that suited me. I hate cold weather and walking in snow that gets into my boots, causing wet socks and frozen toes. I detest carrying wood and having bugs crawl out of it and on to me; of having sawdust from the chain saw get caught in a gust of wind and blown into my eyes and mouth, or drop down a gaping collar, trickling down the inside of my flannel shirt causing me to itch and twitch.

No, when cold weather approaches I retreat to my snug and warm nest and do what I can to avoid getting outside for strenuous activity. No amount of chastising, teasing or attempts to shame me into getting out in the cold will work.

But this winter, really nasty-cold weather came upon us early and suddenly. Our wood pile had grown alarmingly low. What should have lasted until at least January was nearly gone by mid-November. And while we do have a gas furnace, I prefer heat that a wood-burning stove generates, and the fact we're not paying out big bucks annually to the gas company. The idea of actually depending on the furnace for heat filled me with dread.

So on a recent Saturday morning when Bob said we'd ALL be woodcutting that day, I didn't run for cover and drag out my usual pitiful excuses. I knew my help would be needed to work beside Bob and Jenny. Jenny doesn't seem to mind outdoor work; in fact, she even appears to enjoy it. I can't get her to make her bed, but she eagerly will volunteer to help her dad load a pickup with wood and go through a briar patch to do it.

However, Bethany, the opposite of her sister, preferring pursuits which cause no discomfort, sweat, dirt or getting her hair out of place, immediately protested the suggestion that she join the rest of us.

"Why me?" she asked. "You've got enough help. Why do I have to go outside? Why can't we do like the pioneers did with the men doing the woodcutting and the women stay inside and cook and clean house and ....and... make candles!"

We turned in unison to look at her as she waited indignantly for a response. "How many candles have you made lately, Bethany?" I asked.

We were not all happy as we went outdoors to the pickup. Bob was pleased because he had help. Jenny appeared pleased because her sister wasn't. But I wasn't terribly happy about any of it because I could already feel goosebumps raising up the length of my body. I probably wouldn't be warm again until June, I thought.

But the day warmed up as we worked, and I wondered if maybe I might not prefer the day remain cold as I slipped and slid on the thawing ground, my arms loaded with wood, and worried whether we'd even be able to drive out of the remote field in the heavily loaded truck.

The girls, too, seemed to accept that our Saturday was not going to be totally lost and chattered and argued as they grunted under armfuls of wood. Here and there we heard a vocal complaint: "Oooooh gross! This piece of wood landed on a pile of horse manure - well, I'm not gonna touch it!" or "Watch it you moron! You about hit me in the head....Mom, would you tell her something?"

Haven't we got enough wood yet?" I whined to Bob. "Not yet, but soon," he said, "Just let me get this last big limb here." But there always seemed to be another "great big limb." And another.

We talked, chattered and argued as we were watched from a nearby knoll by a bunch of horses. Our cocker spaniel, Mitzi, set up her shrill yipping as a stranger came upon our little group. He looked like a city-guy and was carrying a compound bow. We assumed he was heading out to bow-hunt deer.

"Well, he's not gonna have much luck finding any deer with all the noise Dad is making with the chain saw, is he?" Jenny chortled unsympathetically. And Mitzi's irritating yapping followed the guy down the path.

Finally, driving and bumping over thawing ruts, we headed back home with a cat perched on the back of the seat behind Bob's head. Bethany had forgotten she had a cat snuggled up under her coat until we were halfway to our wood-cutting site, so the kitty had been left in the truck cab while we cut wood; we had just hoped it wouldn't need a sand pile while shut in.

The girls were sitting on the piled-up wood in the back of the pickup as we slid and skidded along. It came to me later as were unloading the wood and working together in relative harmony: Hey, this was sort of fun. I may try it again sometime

Snake *in the* Outhouse

and *Other Stories*

by Linda Banger

Photos by Bob Nandell

Additional copies may be purchased from:

Millstream Publishing
Box 842
Indianola, IA 50125

Book price, $14.95 plus $1.50 shipping & handling.